The Burning Plain

AND OTHER STORIES

THE TEXAS PAN AMERICAN SERIES

International Standard Book Number
0-292-70132-2
Library of Congress Catalog Card Number
67-25698

Eighth paperback printing, 1994

∞   The paper used in this publication meets the
minimum requirements of American National
Standard for Information Sciences—Permanence of
Paper for Printed Library Materials, ANSI Z39.48–1984.

Publication of this book was assisted by a grant
from the Rockefeller Foundation through the Latin
American translation program of the Association of
American University Presses.

CONTENTS

INTRODUCTION

Juan Rulfo is perhaps the best writer of fiction in Latin America today, and a writer to be reckoned with on a universal scale, as his fame continues to spread beyond his native Mexico. If we take soundings here and there of his reputation, in Europe—France, Germany, Spain—or in the countries of South America, we find the critical acclaim swelling constantly.

Born in the state of Jalisco, Mexico, in 1918, Rulfo published his first short stories in the provincial little magazines of Guadalajara in the 1940's. Later on he moved to Mexico City, where the two books which have brought him such celebrity were published: his collection of short stories *El llano en llamas* (1953), translated here, followed by his singular short novel *Pedro Páramo* (1955), which Grove Press brought out in English translation. A second novel, called *La Cordillera*, which Rulfo evidently has been working on for several years, has long been announced as forthcoming by his Mexican publishers.

Most critics of Rulfo's work have concentrated their attention on his brilliant novel *Pedro Páramo*, a bold excursion into modern techniques of writing; however, Rulfo achieves some of his finest moments in the short stories, where the elaboration of a single event or the introspection of a single character allows him to illuminate the meaning, often the utter despair, of a man's life.

Rulfo's world is extremely primitive and profoundly alien to us, at least in its outer aspect, though it is plagued within by the same convulsive agony and fears that strike men's hearts everywhere. The atmosphere is full of repressions and is often mute—a paralytic world seemingly beyond the orbits of time and space. Crude and perverse passions, solitude and death stand out as tangible phenomena against the opaqueness of the Indian characters' tragic lives.

The novels of the Mexican Revolution, beginning with *The Underdogs* (1916) by Mariano Azuela, which dominated the Mexican literary scene for several decades, portrayed a turbulent world where the individual all but disappeared at times. In the 1940's, with such works as Agustín Yáñez's *The Edge of the Storm*, and in the 1950's, with the novels and stories of Carlos Fuentes, Rosario Castellanos, and Juan Rulfo, this collective mask is largely stripped away. The Indians who live and die on the burning Plain in Jalisco are usually treated by Rulfo as individuals with interior lives full of anguish as well as exterior lives of struggle against hardship and abuse. Behind their innocent faces often lurk unspeakable horrors of tragedy and violence: murder, incest, adultery, all the violence of need and desire. These characters seem to live on grief and suffering without friends or love. Indeed, love is an emotion which scarcely appears in these stories, though it plays an important role in *Pedro Páramo*.

Rulfo peels many of his characters down to the core, but some of them, like the landscape, frequently clouded over and hazy, remain blurred, imprecise, and taciturn figures. They are never seen in full face, but always in a silhouette, like the lugubrious, black-garbed crones of "Luvina." The one thing standing forth clear and ubiquitous is death—overpowering life—which seems to hold scant value in this world.

Rulfo has an uncanny feeling for describing the bleak landscape. In the harsh area where his characters live almost nothing stirs or moves, not even buzzards. Life seems to have come to a stop in this paralyzed region, producing a static quality in many of the stories. Macario, for instance, starts out on his rambling monologue, "I am sitting by the sewer waiting for the frogs to come out." And he is still there waiting at the end of the story.

A black, macabre humor of a very special order runs through the collection as a leitmotiv. It is most persistent in "Anacleto Morones," a tale streaked with naturalistic touches: the description of the foetus, and of Pancha's mustache, the vomiting, the women streaming sweat. But the characters' suffering and unhappiness in this bizarre story of a pseudo saint's hypnotic power over ten middle-aged hags occasionally blots out the predominate, acrid humorous tone.

Unlike the novels of the Mexican Revolution and certain Indianist novels of the 1930's, Rulfo's fiction contains no preaching about social abuses, though he refers briefly to the Mexican agrarian question in several stories and sketches the wetback problem most effectively in "El Paso del Norte." Large social ills are commented on dispassionately only when they have bearing on the personal dramas Rulfo is unfolding.

Various techniques which have oriented contemporary fiction along new pathways are present in *The Burning Plain*. Some stories are one long, sustained, interior monologue ("Macario," "We're Very Poor," "Talpa," "Remember"). In "Macario" the past and present mingle chaotically, and frequently the most startling associations of ideas are juxtaposed, strung together by conjunctions which help to paralyze the action and stop the flow of time in the present. Rulfo succeeds in this excellent story in capturing the sickly atmosphere surrounding the idiot boy, who is gnawed by hunger and filled with the terror of hell, and protected, and at the same time exploited, by his Godmother and the servant girl Felipa.

Dialogues are inserted in other stories that are essentially monologues, sustained by the same person who reconstructs situations and scenes from memory ("Luvina," "They've Given Us the Land," "Anacleto Morones"). In "At Daybreak" and "The Man" the action takes place on several levels simultaneously. In the entire collection the pace is slow and sometimes comes to a halt, giving the static effect of eternity that has so caught the critics' attention. As one Mexican commentator aptly declares, there is a triumph of characters over plot, of persons over acts, of the author over time.

In "Talpa"—a classic tale of adultery in which the gripping emotion is not love or desire, but remorse—we are told the outcome of the story at the very beginning. But the suspense, rather than being destroyed by this technique, becomes sharper under Rulfo's dramatic handling. Chronology is broken effectively here, too, and time is immobilized.

A few stories are scarcely more than anecdotes, like "The Night They Left Him Alone," when Feliciano managed to save himself from being hanged like his two unfortunate uncles. Rulfo unfolds this tale in all its dramatic force, pruning away superfluous material, but repeating details and reiterating phrases that give punch to the story.

Rulfo's narratives are composed with the greatest attention to dramatic effects. He knows how to begin a story with a sentence or two of the right cadence to grasp and hold the reader. Urgency, tension, conflict fill the air. For instance, the opening lines of "No

Dogs Bark" set the tone of mystery and doom in a brief dialogue between father and son, a foreboding note swollen with uncertainty that permeates the entire story. The dramatic effect is intensified by the short, agonizing sentences of the dialogue, and the narrative's principal action between the father's words and the son's silence. Here, as in the majority of these stories, the author narrates in a few, brief pages an intense, intimate drama, terse of language, somber in color, with no exterior character description. With remarkable skill Rulfo succeeds in provoking a static impression with his throbbing, dynamic fragments of life.

The technical complexity varies from one story to another: some are relatively simple and develop chronologically, others have different points of view and shifts and shufflings in time. Flashbacks, interior monologues and dialogues with subtle undertones, and an occasional passage of impersonal reflection are employed to give the effect of simultaneity. Time fluctuates among the levels of the present and the causal past, which is vivid in the characters' memories and usually rancorous in its recollections.

The spontaneity of Rulfo's monologues and dialogues is deceptive and points to a conscientious, hard labor on his part to reach this level of stylistic polish. He writes a splendid prose of firm muscularity, its contours never sagging with long patches of commentary. The language is sparse and laconic, unflinchingly realistic, yet charged with poetic qualities. His imagery has a marked rural flavor: earth, rocks, dust, wind, moon, buzzards, coyotes. This imagery never intrudes upon the narrative; it either serves to point up what he is suggesting or else takes on an essential role in the story. In "We're Very Poor" the central image is the river, bringing perdition and ruin in its wake. The river's presence runs through the story, as Rulfo makes us feel its swirling, filthy waters through all our senses. We hear its lapping waves, we smell the stench it leaves as the flood subsides, we witness and shudder at the dirty tears streaming down Tacha's face "as if the river had gotten inside her."

Dominant in Rulfo's stories are the themes of vengeance and death, and the struggle and desire to live. Human nature must always and inevitably assert itself, and in these tales of Biblical power and simplicity it does so convincingly. Rulfo's characters are moved by greed, hate, lust, revenge; they are hampered by fate and beset on all sides by the problems of daily existence. Reality is unendurable but must be faced. Man is abject and lonely. He seeks communication but usually is thwarted. Several stories in the collection, for example, treat the lack of understanding between father and son with particular poignancy. In the domain of violence Rulfo is supreme, and this is all the more impressive as the tone of his writing never becomes rhetorical. It remains calm and measured, pervaded with a classical dignity.

Rulfo's work has immense literary vitality and extraordinary originality. His stories shock and grip us, and many of them make us feel that we are sharing in his characters' pathetic anxiety just to live, to stay alive ("Tell Them Not To Kill Me," "Talpa"). The elements of the harsh physical environment combine with the Mexican Indian's fatalism to forge almost a symbiosis of man and landscape. The parched, dry plain is overwhelming. The Indian accepts life as it is there, and his acts are almost inevitable. He is perpetually in flight, or wracked by fear, mistrust, and remorse, often losing his few cherished possessions and his peace of mind. Impotence and despair reign, and death rattles in the scorching air, the howling wind, the throttling dust of the plain.

G. D. S.

The Burning Plain

AND OTHER STORIES

Macario

I am sitting by the sewer waiting for the frogs to come out. While we were having supper last night they started making a great racket and they didn't stop singing till dawn. Godmother says so too—the cries of the frogs scared her sleep away. And now she would really like to sleep. That's why she ordered me to sit here, by the sewer, with a board in my hand to whack to smithereens every frog that may come hopping out— Frogs are green all over except on the belly. Toads are black. Godmother's eyes are also black. Frogs make good eating. Toads don't. People just don't eat toads. People don't, but I do, and they taste just like frogs. Felipa is the one who says it's bad to eat toads. Felipa has green eyes like a cat's eyes. She feeds me in the kitchen whenever I get to eat. She doesn't want me to hurt frogs. But then Godmother is the one who orders me to do things— I love Felipa more than Godmother. But Godmother is the one who

3

Macario

takes money out of her purse so Felipa can buy all the food. Felipa stays alone in the kitchen cooking food for the three of us. Since I've known her, that's all she does. Washing the dishes is up to me. Carrying in wood for the stove is my job too. Then Godmother is the one who dishes out food to us. After she has eaten, she makes two little piles with her hands, one for Felipa, the other for me. But sometimes Felipa doesn't feel like eating and then the two little piles are for me. That's why I love Felipa, because I'm always hungry and I never get filled up—never, not even when I eat up her food. They say a person does get filled up eating, but I know very well that I don't even though I eat all they give me. And Felipa knows it too— They say in the street that I'm crazy because I never stop being hungry. Godmother has heard them say that. I haven't. Godmother won't let me go out alone on the street. When she takes me out, it's to go to church to hear Mass. There she sets me down next to her and ties my hands with the fringe of her shawl. I don't know why she ties my hands, but she says it's because they say I do crazy things. One day they found me hanging somebody; I was hanging a lady just to be doing it. I don't remember. But then Godmother is the one who says what I do and she never goes about telling lies. When she calls me to eat, it's to give me my part of the food. She's not like other people who invite me to eat with them and then when I get close throw rocks at me until I run away without eating anything. No, Godmother is good to me. That's why I'm content in her house. Besides, Felipa lives here. Felipa is very good to me. That's why I love her— Felipa's milk is as sweet as hibiscus flowers. I've drunk goat's milk and also the milk of a sow that had recently had pigs. But no, it isn't as good as Felipa's milk— Now it's been a long time since she has let me nurse the breasts that she has where we just have ribs, and where there comes out, if you know how to get it, a better milk than the one Godmother gives us for lunch on Sundays— Felipa used to come every night to the room where I sleep, and snuggle up to me, leaning over me or a little to one side. Then she would fix her breasts so that I could suck the sweet, hot milk that came out in streams on my tongue— Many times I've eaten hibiscus flowers to try to forget my hunger. And Felipa's milk had the same flavor, except that I liked it better because, at the same time that she let me nurse, Felipa would tickle me all over. Then almost always she would stay there sleeping by me until dawn. And that was very good for me, because I didn't worry about the cold and I wasn't afraid of being damned to hell if I died there alone some night— Sometimes I'm not so afraid of hell. But sometimes I am. And then I like to scare myself about going to hell any day now, because my head is so hard and I like to bang it against the first thing I come across. But Felipa comes and scares away my fears. She tickles me with her hands like she knows how to do and she stops that fear of mine that I have of dying. And for a little while I even forget it— Felipa says, when she feels like being with me, that she will tell the Lord all my sins. She will go to heaven very soon and will talk with Him, asking Him to pardon me for all the great wickedness that fills my body from head to toe. She will tell Him to pardon me so I won't worry about it any more. That's why she goes to confession every day. Not because she's bad, but because I'm full of devils inside, and she has to drive them out of my body by confessing for me. Every single day. Every single afternoon of every single day. She will do that favor for me her whole life. That's what Felipa says. That's why I love her so much— Still, having a head so hard is the great thing. I bang it against the pillars of the corridor hours on end and nothing happens to it. It stands banging and doesn't crack. I bang it against the floor—first slowly, then harder—and that sounds like a drum. Just like the drum that goes with the wood flute when I hear them through the window of the church, tied to Godmother, and hearing outside the boom boom of the drum— And Godmother says that if there are chinches and cockroaches and scorpions in my room it's because I'm going to burn in hell if I keep on with this business of banging my head on the floor. But what I like is to hear the drum. She should know that. Even when I'm in church, waiting to go out soon into the street to see why the drum is heard from so far away, deep inside the church and above the damning of the priest— "The road of good things is filled with light. The road of bad things is dark." That's what the priest says— I get up and go out of my room while it's still dark. I sweep the street and I go back in my room before daylight grabs me. On the street things happen. There are lots of people who will hit me on the head with rocks as soon as they see me. Big sharp rocks rain from every side. And then my shirt has to be mended and I have to wait many days for the scabs on my face or knees to heal. And go through having my hands tied again, because if I don't they'll hurry to scratch off the scabs and a stream of blood will come out again. Blood has a good flavor too, although it isn't really like the flavor of Felipa's milk— That's why I always live shut up in my house—so they won't throw rocks at me. As soon as they feed me I lock myself in my room and bar the door so my sins won't find me out, because it's dark. And I don't even light the torch to see where the cockroaches are climbing on me. Now I keep quiet. I go to bed on my sacks, and as soon as I feel a cockroach walking along my neck with its scratchy feet I give it a slap with my hand and squash it. But I don't light the torch. I'm not going to let my sins catch me off guard with my torch lit looking for cockroaches under my blanket— Cockroaches pop like firecrackers when you mash them. I don't know whether crickets pop. I never kill crickets. Felipa says that crickets always make noise so you can't hear the cries of souls suffering in purgatory. The day there are no more crickets the world will be filled with the screams of holy souls and we'll all start running scared out of our wits. Besides, I like very much to prick my ears up and listen to the noise of the crickets. There are lots of them in my room. Maybe there are more crickets than cockroaches among the folds of the sacks where I sleep. There are scorpions too. Every once in a while they fall from the ceiling and I have to hold my breath until they've made their way across me to reach the floor. Because if an arm moves or one of my bones begins to tremble, I feel the burn of the sting right away. That hurts. Once Felipa got stung on the behind by one of them. She started moaning and making soft little cries to the Holy Virgin that her behind wouldn't be ruined. I rubbed spit on her. All night I spent rubbing spit on her and praying with her, and after a while, when I saw that my spit wasn't making her any better, I also helped her to cry with my eyes all that I could— Anyway, I like it better in my room than out on the street, attracting the attention of those who love to throw rocks at people. Here nobody does anything to me. Godmother doesn't even scold me when she sees me eating up her hibiscus flowers, or her myrtles, or her pomegranates. She knows how awfully hungry I am all the time. She knows that I'm always hungry. She knows that no meal is enough to fill up my insides, even though I go about snitching things to eat here and there all the time. She knows that I gobble up the chick-pea slop I give to

Macario

the fat pigs and the dry-corn slop I give to the skinny pigs. So she knows how hungry I go around from the time I get up until the time I go to bed. And as long as I find something to eat here in this house I'll stay here. Because I think that the day I quit eating I'm going to die, and then I'll surely go straight to hell. And nobody will get me out of there, not even Felipa, who is so good to me, or the scapular that Godmother gave to me and that I wear hung around my neck— Now I'm by the sewer waiting for the frogs to come out. And not one has come out all this while I've been talking. If they take much longer to come out I may go to sleep and then there won't be any way to kill them and Godmother won't be able to sleep at all if she hears them singing and she'll get very angry. And then she'll ask one of that string of saints she has in her room to send the devils after me, to take me off to eternal damnation, right now, without even passing through purgatory, and then I won't be able to see my papa or mamma, because that's where they are— So I just better keep on talking— What I would really like to do is take a few swallows of Felipa's milk, that good milk as sweet as honey that comes from under the hibiscus flowers—

They gave us the land

After walking so many hours without coming across even the shadow of a tree, or a seedling of a tree, or any kind of root, we hear dogs barking.

At times, along this road with no edges, it seemed like there'd be nothing afterward, that nothing could be found on the other side, at the end of this plain split with cracks and dry arroyos. But there is something. There's a town. You can hear the dogs barking and smell the smoke in the air, and you relish that smell of people as if it was a hope.

But the town is still far off. It's the wind that brings it close.

We've been walking since dawn. Now it's something like four in the afternoon. Somebody looks up at the sky, strains his eyes to where the sun hangs, and says, "It's about four o'clock."

That was Melitón. Faustino, Esteban, and I are with him. There are four of us. I count them: two in front, and two behind. I look

They gave us the land

further back and don't see anybody. Then I say to myself, "There are four of us." Not long ago, at about eleven, there were over twenty, but little by little they've been scattering away until just this knot of us is left.

Faustino says, "It may rain."

We all lift our faces and look at a heavy black cloud passing over our heads. And we think, "Maybe so."

We don't say what we're thinking. For some time now we haven't felt like talking. Because of the heat. Somewhere else we'd talk with pleasure, but here it's difficult. You talk here and the words get hot in your mouth with the heat from outside, and they dry up on your tongue until they take your breath away. That's the way things are here. That's why nobody feels like talking.

A big fat drop of water falls, making a hole in the earth and leaving a mark like spit. It's the only one that falls. We wait for others to fall and we roll our eyes looking for them. But there are no others. It isn't raining. Now if you look at the sky, you'll see the rain cloud moving off real fast in the distance. The wind that comes from the town pushes the cloud against the blue shadows of the hills. And the drop of water which fell here by mistake is gobbled up by the thirsty earth.

Who the devil made this plain so big? What's it good for, anyway?

We started walking again; we'd stopped to watch it rain. It didn't rain. Now we start walking again. It occurs to me that we've walked more than the ground we've covered. That occurs to me. If it had rained, perhaps other things would've occurred to me. Anyway, I know that ever since I was a boy I've never seen it rain out on the plain—what you would really call rain.

No, the plain is no good for anything. There're no rabbits or birds. There's nothing. Except a few scrawny huizache trees and a patch or two of grass with the blades curled up; if it weren't for them, there wouldn't be anything.

And here we are. The four of us on foot. Before, we used to ride on horseback and carry a rifle slung over our shoulder. Now we don't even carry the rifle.

I've always thought that taking away our rifles was a good thing. Around these parts it's dangerous to go around armed. You can get killed without warning if you're seen with your thirty-thirty strapped on. But horses are another matter. If we'd come on horses we would already be tasting the green river water, and walking our full stomachs around the streets of the town to settle our dinner. We'd already have done that if we still had all those horses. But they took away our horses with the rifles.

I turn in every direction and look at the plain. So much land all for nothing. Your eyes slide when they don't find anything to light on. Just a few lizards stick their heads out of their holes, and as soon as they feel the roasting sun quickly hide themselves again in the small shade of a rock. But when we have to work here, what can we do to keep cool from the sun?—because they gave us this crust of rocky ground for planting.

They told us, "From the town up to here belongs to you."

We asked, "The Plain?"

"Yes, the plain. All the Big Plain."

We opened our mouths to say that we didn't want the plain, that we wanted what was by the river. From the river up to where, through the meadows, the trees called casuarinas are, and the pastures and the good land. Not this tough cow's hide they call the Plain.

But they didn't let us say these things. The official hadn't come

They gave us the land

to converse with us. He put the papers in our hands and told us, "Don't be afraid to have so much land just for yourselves."

"But the Plain, sir—"

"There are thousands and thousands of plots of land."

"But there's no water. There's not even a mouthful of water."

"How about the rainy season? Nobody told you you'd get irrigated land. As soon as it rains out there, the corn will spring up as if you were pulling it."

"But, sir, the earth is all washed away and hard. We don't think the plow will cut into the earth of the Plain that's like a rock quarry. You'd have to make holes with a pick-axe to plant the seed, and even then you can't be sure that anything will come up; no corn or anything else will come up."

"You can state that in writing. And now you can go. You should be attacking the large-estate owners and not the government that is giving you the land."

"Wait, sir. We haven't said anything against the Center. It's all against the Plain— You can't do anything when there's nothing to work with— That's what we're saying— Wait and let us explain. Look, we'll start back where we were—"

But he refused to listen to us.

So they've given us this land. And in this sizzling frying pan they want us to plant some kind of seeds to see if something will take root and come up. But nothing will come up here. Not even buzzards. You see them out here once in a while, very high, flying fast, trying to get away as soon as possible from this hard white earth, where nothing moves and where you walk as if losing ground.

Melitón says, "This is the land they've given us."

Faustino says, "What?"

I don't say anything. I think, Melitón doesn't have his head

screwed on right. It must be the heat that makes him talk like that
—the heat that's cut through his hat and made his head hot. And
if not, why does he say what he's saying? What land have they
given us, Melitón? There isn't even enough here for the wind to
blow up a dust cloud.

Melitón says again, "It must be good for something—for something, even just for running mares."

"What mares?" Esteban asks him.

I hadn't noticed Esteban very closely. Now that he's speaking
I notice him. He's wearing a coat that reaches down to his navel,
and under his coat something that looks like a hen's head is peering out.

Yes, it's a red hen that Esteban is carrying under his coat. You
can see her sleepy eyes and open beak as if she was yawning. I
ask him, "Hey, Teban, where'd you pick up that hen?"

"She's mine!" he says.

"You didn't have her before. Where'd you buy her, huh?"

"I didn't buy her, she's from my chickenyard."

"Then you brought her for food, didn't you?"

"No, I brought her along to take care of her. Nobody was left
at my house to feed her; that's why I brought her. Whenever I
go anyplace very far I take her along."

"Hidden there she's going to smother. Better bring her out in
the air."

He places her under his arm and blows the hot air from his
mouth on her. Then he says, "We're reaching the cliff."

I don't hear what Esteban is saying any more. We've got in line
to go down the barranca and he's at the very front. He has a hold
of the hen by her legs and he swings her to and fro so he won't
hit her head against the rocks.

They gave us the land

As we descend, the land becomes good. A cloud of dust rises from us as if we were a mule train descending, but we like getting all dusty. We like it. After tromping for eleven hours on the hard plain, we're pleased to be wrapped in that thing that jumps over us and tastes like earth.

Above the river, over the green tops of the casuarina trees, fly flocks of green chachalacas. That's something else we like.

Now we can hear the dogs barking, near us, because the wind coming from the town re-echoes in the barranca and fills it with all its noises.

Esteban clutches his hen to him again when we approach the first houses. He unties her legs so she can shake off the numbness, and then he and his hen disappear behind some tepemezquite trees.

"Here's where I stop off," Esteban tells us.

We move on further into town.

The land they've given us is back up yonder.

The Hill of the Comadres

The Torricos—they're dead now—were always good friends of mine. Maybe in Zapotlán they weren't liked, but as far as I'm concerned they were always good friends, until shortly before they died. Now the fact that they weren't liked in Zapotlán doesn't mean a thing, because I wasn't liked there either, and I understand that the people of Zapotlán never had much use for any of us who lived on the Hill. This dates from way back.

On the other hand, at the Hill of the Comadres the Torricos didn't get along well with everybody either. There were constant quarrels. And—if I'm not exaggerating—they owned the land there and the houses on the land, even though when the land was distributed most of the Hill had been divided equally among the sixty of us who lived there, and the Torricos got just a piece of land with a maguey field, but where most of the houses were scattered. In spite of that, the Hill of the Comadres belonged to the Torricos. The piece of ground I worked belonged to Odilón and Remigio Torrico too, and the dozen and a half green hills you

15

could see down below were theirs. There was no reason to check on anything. Everybody knew that's the way it was.

But from then on people began leaving the Hill of the Comadres. From time to time somebody would leave—they would cross the cattle guard where the high post is, disappear among the oaks, and never return again. They left, that's all.

And I too would've been very glad to go see what was behind that hill that didn't let anybody come back, but I liked the Hill, and besides, I was a good friend of the Torricos.

The piece of ground where I planted a little corn every year, and also beans, was on the uphill side, where the slope runs down to that barranca called Bull's Head.

It wasn't a bad place, but the earth got sticky as soon as it started to rain, and then too a large stretch of ground was full of hard, sharp rocks as big as tree trunks that seemed to get bigger with time. But the corn grew well and the ears of corn were very sweet. The Torricos, who always had to put salt on everything they ate, didn't need to put any on my ears of corn; they never looked for salt or talked about putting any on the corn I grew at the Bull's Head.

In spite of all that, in spite of the fact that the green hills down below were the best, the people kept on leaving. They didn't go to Zapotlán, but in this other direction, from where the wind blows in full of the smell of oaks and the sounds of the mountain. They left silently, without saying anything or fighting with anybody. They sure felt like fighting the Torricos to get even with them for all the bad things they'd done to them, but they didn't have the courage. That's the way it was.

Still, after the Torricos died nobody came back here any more. I was waiting for them. But nobody came back. At first I looked after their houses; I mended their roofs and I put branches in the holes in their walls; but when I saw they weren't coming back, I quit doing it. What always did come were the downpours in the middle of the year, and those heavy winds that blow in February and whip your sarape off you. Every now and then, too, the crows came flying very low and cawing in a loud voice, as if they thought they were in some deserted place.

So things went on like that even after the Torricos were dead.

From here, where I'm sitting now, you used to be able to see Zapotlán clearly. At any hour of the day or night you could see the little white speck that was Zapotlán far away. But now the ja-rillas have grown up real thick and no matter how much the wind moves them from one side to another you can't see anything through them.

I remember how the Torricos used to come sit here too, squatting for hours and hours until dark, looking down there without getting tired, as if this place stirred up their thoughts or gave them a hankering to go in and have a good time in Zapotlán. Only afterward I found out they didn't think about that. They just looked at the road—that wide, sandy track you could follow with your eyes from the beginning until it got lost among the pines on Half Moon Hill.

I never knew anybody who could see as far as Remigio Torrico. He had one eye. But the black and half-closed eye that was good seemed to bring things so close that they were almost at his hands' reach. So he had no trouble making out what objects were moving on the road. And when his eye lit on something that pleased him, the two of them got up from their lookout and disappeared from the Hill of the Comadres for a while.

That was the time when everything changed around here. The

17

people brought their animals out of the caves in the hills and tied them up in their corrals. Then we found out that they had sheep and turkeys. And it was easy to see how many piles of corn and yellow squash were out in the sun of the patio each morning. The wind crossing the mountains was colder than usual; but nobody knew why—everyone said the weather was fine. And you could hear the roosters crowing in the early morning, like in any peaceful village, and it seemed as if there'd always been peace on the Hill of the Comadres.

Then the Torricos came back. You knew they were coming before they got there, because their dogs ran out to meet them barking the whole way. And just by the barking everybody calculated the distance and the direction in which they'd come. Then everybody hurried to hide all their things again.

Every time the Torricos came back to the Hill of the Comadres, this was the kind of fear they spread.

But I was never afraid of them. I was a good friend of both of them and sometimes I wished I wasn't quite so old, so I could join them in what they were up to. But I wasn't good for much any more. I realized that the night I helped them rob a mule driver. That's when I realized I haven't got it any more—like the life I had in me had been used up and couldn't take any more strain. That's what I realized.

It was about the middle of the rainy season when the Torricos invited me to help them bring back sacks of sugar. I was kind of scared. First, because it was pouring down rain—one of those storms where the water seems to wash the ground right from under your feet. Afterwards, because I didn't know where I was going. Anyway, I realized then that I was no longer in shape for such outings.

The Hill of the Comadres

The Torricos told me the place we were going to wasn't far. "In about a quarter of an hour we'll be there," they told me. But when we reached the Half Moon road it began to get dark and when we got to where the mule driver was it was well into the night.

The mule driver didn't get up to see who was coming. No doubt he was waiting for the Torricos and that's why seeing us arrive didn't surprise him. That's what I thought. But during all the time we were carting the sugar sacks back and forth, the mule driver was quiet, sprawling in the grass. Then I told the Torricos that. I said to them, "That one stretched out there seems to be dead or something."

"No, he must be asleep, that's all," they said to me. "We left him here to watch, but he must have got tired of waiting and gone to sleep."

I went and gave him a kick in the ribs so he'd wake up, but he didn't budge.

"He's good and dead," I said to them again.

"No, don't believe it. He's just a little stunned because Odilón hit him on the head with a stick of wood; later on he'll get up. You'll see, as soon as the sun comes out and he feels the warmth he'll get right up and go straight home. Grab that sack there and let's get going!" That's all he said to me.

Finally I gave the dead man a last kick, and it sounded just like I'd kicked a dry tree trunk. Then I hoisted the bundle on my shoulder and went on ahead. The Torricos followed me. I heard them singing for a long time, until dawn. When it got light I didn't hear them any more. The breeze that blows a little before dawn carried away the cries of their song and I couldn't tell any more if they were following me, until I heard the barking of their dogs on all sides.

The Hill of the Comadres

That's how I found out what the Torricos came looking for every afternoon when they sat by my house at the Hill of the Comadres.

I killed Remigio Torrico.

That was when only a few people were left among the ranches here. At first they left one by one, but the last ones were almost going in droves. They made some money and they left when the frosts came. In past years the frosts came and destroyed the crops in a single night. And this year too. That's why they left. No doubt they believed that the following year would be the same thing, and I guess they no longer felt like putting up with the terrible weather every year and the terrible Torricos all the time.

So when I killed Remigio Torrico there weren't any people any more on the Hill of the Comadres or in the surrounding hills.

This happened along about October. I remember there was a real big moon with lots of light, because I sat down outside my house to mend a sack that was full of holes, using the good moonlight, when Torrico arrived.

He must've been drunk. He stood in front of me and staggered from one side to the other, cutting off the light I needed from the moon.

"It isn't right to do things in a sneaky way," he said to me after some time. "I like things straight, and if you don't, too bad for you, because I've come here to straighten them out."

I went on mending my sack. I was giving all my attention to sewing up the holes, and the harness needle worked very well when the moonlight shone on it. That's why he must've thought I wasn't listening to what he said.

"I'm talking to you," he shouted at me, now real mad. "You know damned well why I've come."

I got a little scared when he came close and shouted that almost in my face. But I tried to see his face to be sure how mad he was and I kept on looking at him, as if asking him why he'd come.

That had its effect. Now a little calmed down, he let loose saying that with people like me one had to catch them off their guard.

"My mouth gets dry talking to you after what you did," he said to me, "but my brother was as good a friend of mine as you and that's the only reason I've come to see you, to see how you'll explain Odilón's death."

I listened to him very carefully now. I laid the sack to one side and listened without doing anything else.

I found out how he blamed me for killing his brother. But it hadn't been me. I remembered who did it, and I would've told him, but it looked like he wouldn't give me a chance to tell him the way things were.

"Odilón and I fought a lot," he went on saying. "He was kind of slow to catch on to things and he liked to fight with everybody, but that's as far as it went. After a few blows he'd calm down. And that's what I want to know: if he said something to you, or tried to take something away from you, or what it was that happened. Maybe he tried to hit you and you beat him to it. Something like that must've happened."

I shook my head to tell him no, that I had nothing to do with it.

"Listen," Torrico cut me short, "Odilón had fourteen pesos in his shirt pocket that day. When I lifted him up I searched him and I didn't find the fourteen pesos. Then I found out yesterday that you'd bought a blanket."

That was true. I had bought myself a blanket. I saw how the cold weather was coming on us fast and the overcoat I had was all in rags; that was why I went to Zapotlán to get a blanket. But to do that I'd sold the two goats I had, and it wasn't with Odilón's fourteen pesos that I bought it. He could see the sack had got full of holes because I had to carry the little kid goat in it, because it couldn't walk yet like I wanted it to.

"You might as well know once and for all that I intend to get even with them for what they did to Odilón, whoever killed him. And I know who it was," I heard him say right above my head.

"So it was me?" I asked him.

"And who else? Odilón and I were hoodlums or whatever you want to call us, and I won't say we never killed anybody, but we never did it for such small pickings. That's what I'm telling you."

The big October moon shone full over the corral and cast Remigio's long shadow onto the wall of my house. I saw him moving in the direction of a hawthorn tree and grab the machete that I always kept there. Then I saw him coming back with the machete in his hand.

But when he moved away from in front of me, the moonlight shone brightly on the harness needle I'd stuck in the sack. And I don't know why, but suddenly I began to have great faith in that needle. That's why, when Remigio Torrico came up to my side, I pulled out the needle and without waiting for anything stabbed him with it near his navel. I plunged it in as far as it would go. And I left it there.

Right away he twisted up like when you have stomach cramps and he began to twitch until he was doubled up on his legs, seated on the ground, all weak and with his one eye filled with fear.

For a moment it looked like he was going to straighten up and give me a blow with the machete; but I guess he changed his mind or didn't know how to do it, for he dropped the machete and twisted up again. That's all.

Then I saw him looking sad, as if he was beginning to feel sick. It'd been a long time since I'd seen such a sad look and I felt sorry for him. That's why I pulled out the needle from his belly and stuck it in higher up, where I thought his heart must be. And, yes, that's where it was, because he just gave two or three jerks like a chicken with its head chopped off and then he was still.

He must've been dead when I said to him: "Look, Remigio, you've got to pardon me, but I didn't kill Odilón. It was the Alcaraces. I was there when he died, but I remember very well that I didn't kill him. It was the whole Alcaraz family that did it. They all jumped him, and when I realized what was happening Odilón was dying. And, you know why? First because Odilón shouldn't have gone to Zapotlán. You know that. Sooner or later something was bound to happen to him in that town, where so many people had reason to remember all about him. And the Alcaraces didn't like him either. You don't know any better than I why he went there to get mixed up with them.

"It all happened sudden like. I had just bought my sarape and was going out when your brother spat a mouthful of mescal in the face of one of the Alcaraces. He did it just for fun. You could see he'd done it for fun, because he made them all laugh. But they were all drunk—Odilón and the Alcaraces and everybody. And suddenly they all jumped him. They took out their knives and they rushed at him and stabbed him until there wasn't any life left in Odilón. That's how he died.

"So you see, it wasn't me who killed him. I'd like you to know that I didn't have a thing to do with it."

That's what I said to the dead Remigio.

The moon had already gone down behind the other side of the oaks when I returned to the Hill of the Comadres with my empty market basket. But first I dipped it several times into the stream to wash off the blood. I was going to need it right along and I didn't want to see Remigio's blood on it every time.

I remember that it happened about in October, during the fiesta in Zapotlán. And I say I remember it was during those days because in Zapotlán they were firing rockets, and every time a rocket went off out in the direction where I dumped Remigio a great flock of buzzards rose up.

That's what I remember.

We're very poor

Everything is going from bad to worse here. Last week my Aunt Jacinta died, and on Saturday, when we'd already buried her and we started getting over the sadness, it began raining like never before. That made my father mad, because the whole rye harvest was stacked out in the open, drying in the sun. And the cloudburst came all of a sudden in great waves of water, without giving us time to get in even a handful; all we could do at our house was stay huddled together under the roof, watching how the cold water falling from the sky ruined that yellow rye so recently harvested.

And only yesterday, when my sister Tacha just turned twelve, we found out that the cow my father had given her for her birthday had been swept away by the river.

The river started rising three nights ago, about dawn. I was asleep, but the noise the river was making woke me up right away

We're very poor

and made me jump out of bed and grab my blanket, as if the roof of our house was falling in. But then I went back to sleep, because I recognized the sound of the river, and that sound went on and on the same until I fell asleep again.

When I got up, the morning was full of black clouds and it looked like it had been raining without letup. The noise the river made kept getting closer and louder. You could smell it, like you smell a fire, the rotting smell of backwater.

When I went out to take a look, the river had already gone over its banks. It was slowly rising along the main street and was rushing into the house of that woman called La Tambora. You could hear the gurgling of the water when it entered her yard and when it poured out the door in big streams. La Tambora rushed in and out through what was already a part of the river, shooing her hens out into the street so they'd hide some place where the current couldn't reach them.

On the other side, where the bend is, the river must've carried off—who knows when—the tamarind tree in my Aunt Jacinta's yard, because now you can't see any tamarind. It was the only one in the village, and that's the reason why people realize this flood we're having is the biggest one that's gone down the river in many years.

My sister and I went back in the afternoon to look at that mountain of water that kept getting thicker and darker and was now way above where the bridge should be. We stood there for hours and hours without getting tired, just looking at it. Then we climbed up the ravine, because we wanted to hear what people were saying, for down below, by the river, there's a rumbling noise, and you just see lots of mouths opening and shutting like they wanted to say something, but you don't hear anything. That's why we climbed up the ravine, where other people are watching the river and telling each other about the damage it's done. That's where we found out the river had carried off La Serpentina, the cow that belonged to my sister Tacha because my father gave it to her on her birthday, and it had one white ear and one red ear and very pretty eyes.

I still don't understand why La Serpentina got it into her head to cross the river when she knew it wasn't the same river she was used to every day. La Serpentina was never so flighty. What probably happened is she must've been asleep to have let herself get drowned like that. Lots of times I had to wake her up when I opened the corral gate for her, because if I hadn't she would've stayed there all day long with her eyes shut, real quiet and sighing, like you hear cows sighing when they're asleep.

What must've happened then was that she went to sleep. Maybe she woke up when she felt the heavy water hit her flanks. Maybe then she got scared and tried to turn back; but when she started back she probably got confused and got a cramp in that water, black and hard as sliding earth. Maybe she bellowed for help. Only God knows how she bellowed.

I asked a man who saw the river wash her away if he hadn't seen the calf that was with her. But the man said he didn't know whether he'd seen it. He only said that a spotted cow passed by with her legs in the air very near where he was standing and then she turned over and he didn't see her horns or her legs or any sign of her again. Lots of tree trunks with their roots and everything were floating down the river and he was very busy fishing out firewood, so he couldn't be sure whether they were animals or trunks going by.

That's why we don't know whether the calf is alive, or if it went

We're very poor

down the river with its mother. If it did, may God watch over them both.

What we're upset about in my house is what may happen any day, now that my sister Tacha is left without anything. My father went to a lot of trouble to get hold of La Serpentina when she was a heifer to give to my sister, so she would have a little capital and not become a bad woman like my two older sisters did.

My father says they went bad because we were poor in my house and they were very wild. From the time they were little girls they were sassy and difficult. And as soon as they grew up they started going out with the worst kind of men, who taught them bad things. They learned fast and they soon caught on to the whistles calling them late at night. Later on they even went out during the daytime. They kept going down to the river for water and sometimes, when you'd least expect it, there they'd be out in the yard, rolling around on the ground, all naked, and each one with a man on top of her.

Then my father ran them both off. At first he put up with them as long as he could, but later on he couldn't take it any more and he threw them out into the street. They went to Ayutla and I don't know where else; but they're bad women.

That's why father is so upset now about Tacha—because he doesn't want her to go the way of her two sisters. He realized how poor she is with the loss of her cow, seeing that she has nothing left to count on while she's growing up so as to marry a good man who will always love her. And that's going to be hard now. When she had the cow it was a different story, for somebody would've had the courage to marry her, just to get that fine cow.

Our only hope left is that the calf is still alive. I hope to God it didn't try to cross the river behind its mother. Because if it did,

then my sister Tacha is just one step from becoming a bad woman. And Mamma doesn't want her to.

My mother can't understand why God has punished her so giving her daughters like that, when in her family, from Grandma on down, there have never been bad people. They were all raised in the fear of God and were very obedient and were never disrespectful to anybody. That's the way they all were. Who knows where those two daughters of hers got that bad example. She can't remember. She goes over and over all her memories and she can't see clearly where she went wrong or why she had one daughter after another with the same bad ways. She can't remember any such example. And every time she thinks about them she cries and says, "May God look after the two of them."

But my father says there's nothing to be done about them now. The one in danger is the one still at home, Tacha, who is shooting up like a rod and whose breasts are beginning to fill out, promising to be like her sisters'—high and pointed, the kind that bounce about and attract attention.

"Yes," he says, "they'll catch the eye of anyone who sees them. And she'll end up going bad; mark my words, she'll end up bad."

That's why my father is so upset.

And Tacha cries when she realizes her cow won't come back because the river killed her. She's here at my side in her pink dress, looking at the river from the ravine, and she can't stop crying. Streams of dirty water run down her face as if the river had gotten inside her.

I put my arms around her trying to comfort her, but she doesn't understand. She cries even more. A noise comes out of her mouth like the river makes near its banks, which makes her tremble and shake all over, and the whole time the river keeps on rising. The drops of stinking water from the river splash Tacha's wet face, and her two little breasts bounce up and down without stopping, as if suddenly they were beginning to swell, to start now on the road to ruin.

The man

The man's feet sank into the sand, leaving a formless track, like some animal's hoof. They clambered over the rocks, digging in at the steepness of the ascent, then they trudged on upward, searching out the horizon.

"Flat feet," said the one who was following him. "With a toe missing. The big toe on his left foot. There aren't many around like that. So it'll be easy."

The path, filled with thorns and thistles, climbed up between patches of grass. It was so narrow it seemed like an ant's path. It climbed without stopping toward the sky. There it became lost and then appeared further on, under a more distant sky.

His feet followed the path without straying from it. The man walked resting his weight on his callused heels, scraping the rocks with his toenails, scratching his arms, stopping at each horizon to measure his goal: *"Not mine, but his,"* he said. And he turned his head to see who had spoken.

The man

Not a drop of air, only the noise he had made echoing among the broken branches. Weary from having to grope his way, calculating each step, with bated breath, he repeated: *"That's all I'm going to do."* And he knew then that he had spoken.

"He climbed along here, raking the mountainside," said the man pursuing him. "He cut away branches with a machete. You can tell that he was gripped by fear. Fear always leaves marks. That's what will cause his downfall."

His courage began to wane when the hours stretched out and behind one horizon loomed another and the mountain he was scaling never came to an end. He took out his machete and cut the branches tough as roots and slashed the grass down to the roots. He chewed on a slimy mess and spat it out angrily on the ground. He sucked his teeth and spat again. The sky above was calm and quiet, its clouds showing translucent between the silhouette of the leafless calabash trees. It wasn't the season for leaves. It was that dry and scabby season of thorns and dry wild spikes. Anxiously he hacked at the thickets of shrubs with his machete: *"It will get dull doing this kind of work, better leave things in peace."*

He heard his own voice there behind.

"His own anger gave him away," said the pursuer. "He has told us who he is, now all we need to know is where he is. I'll climb up where he climbed, then I'll go down where he went down, following his tracks until I tire him out. And he'll be where I stop. He'll get down on his knees and ask me to forgive him. And I'll let him have a bullet in the back of his neck— That's what will happen when I find you."

He reached the end. Just pure sky, ashen, half-burned by the dark cloud of night. The earth had fallen over to the other side. He looked at the house before him, with the last smoke from the embers coming from it. He sank into the soft, recently plowed earth. Unwittingly, he touched the door with the handle of his machete. A dog came and licked his knees, another one ran around him, wagging its tail. Then he pushed open the door, closed only to the night.

The one pursuing him said: "He did a good job. Didn't even wake them up. He must have arrived by one o'clock, the hour when you are soundest asleep; after the 'Rest in peace,' when life slips into the hands of night and when the body's tiredness wears away the cords of distrust and breaks them."

"*I shouldn't have killed all of them,*" said the man. "*At least not all of them.*" That was all he said.

The dawn was gray and filled with cold air. He went down the other side, slipping along the grass. He threw down the machete that he was still clutching when the cold stiffened his hands. He left it there. He saw it shine like a piece of lifeless snake among the dry spikes.

Far below, the river flows, its waters lapping at the flowering cypresses, rocking its thick current in silence. It twists and turns upon itself. It winds like a serpent coiled on the green earth. It makes no noise. You could sleep there, near it, and someone would hear your breathing, but not the river's. Ivy trails down from the tall cypresses and sinks into the water, joining its hands together and forming cobwebs that the river never unweaves.

The man found the river's course by the yellow color of the cypresses. He didn't hear it. He just saw it twisting under the shadows. He saw the chachalacas come. The afternoon before they had been following the sun, flying in flocks behind the light. Now the sun was about to come out and they were returning again.

He crossed himself three times. "Forgive me," he said to them.

And he began his work. When he got to the third one, tears streamed down his face. Or maybe it was sweat. It is hard work to kill. The hide is slippery. It defends itself even though resigned to defeat. And the machete was dull: "You must forgive me," he said to them again.

"He sat down on the sand of the beach," said the pursuer. "He sat down here and didn't move for a long time. He waited for the clouds to go away. But the sun didn't come out that day or the next. I remember. It was on that Sunday when my newborn baby died and we went to bury it. We weren't sad. All I remember is that the sky was gray and the flowers we were carrying were faded and drooping as if they felt the sun's absence.

"That man stayed here, waiting. There were his tracks—the nest he made near the underbrush, the warmth of his body making a hole in the wet earth."

"I shouldn't have left the path," thought the man. *"I would've been there by now. But it's dangerous to go where everyone goes, especially with this load I'm carrying. Anyone looking at me must see this weight, just as if it was a strange swelling. That's the way it feels to me. When I felt them cut off my toe, they saw it but I didn't until later. And so now, although I don't want to, I have to have some sign. That's the way I feel, because of the weight, or maybe the effort tired me out."* Then he added: *"I shouldn't have killed all of them; I should've been satisfied with the one I had to kill; but it was dark and the shapes were the same size— After all, with so many at once it won't cost as much to bury them."*

"You'll get tired before I do. I'll get where you want to get before you do," said the one who was following him. "I know your intentions by heart, who you are and where you're from and where you're going. I'll get there before you do."

The man

"*This is not the place,*" said the man when he saw the river. "*I'll cross it here and then further on and maybe come out on the same bank. I have to be on the other side, where they don't know me, where I've never been and nobody knows about me; then I'll go straight until I get there. Nobody will ever get me out of there.*"

More flocks of chachalacas passed by, screeching with deafening cries.

"*I'll go further down. The river's a tangle of bends here and might bring me back where I don't want to go.*"

"Nobody will hurt you, son. I'm here to protect you. That's why I was born before you were and my bones hardened before yours."

He heard his voice, his own voice, slowly coming from his mouth. He heard the noise it made, like a false and senseless thing.

Why would he have said that? Now his son must be making fun of him. Or maybe not. "Maybe he's full of bitterness against me for leaving him alone in our last hour. Because it was mine too; just mine. He came after me. He wasn't looking for you; it was just me he was after, my face the one he dreamed of seeing dead, rubbed in the mud, kicked and tromped on until it was disfigured. Just like I did to his brother; but I did it face to face, José Alcancía, facing him and you, and all you did was cry and tremble with fear. Since then I knew who you were and how you would come looking for me. I waited a month for you, awake day and night, knowing you would come crawling, hidden like an evil snake. And you came late. And I came late too. I arrived after you. The burial of my baby delayed me. Now I understand. Now I understand why the flowers wilted in my hand."

"*I shouldn't have killed all of them,*" the man was thinking. "*It wasn't worth it putting such a burden on my back. Dead people weigh more than live ones; they crush you. I should've felt them*

The man

one by one until I found him; I would've known him by his mus-
tache; even if it was dark I would've known where to strike him
before he could get up— After all, the way it was was better. No-
body will cry for them and I'll live in peace. The thing now is to
find the way out of here before night catches me."

In the afternoon the man got to the narrow part of the river. The
sun hadn't come out all day, but there was light moving the
shadows about; that's how he knew it was afternoon.

"You're caught," said the one following him, who was now sitting on the river bank. "You've come to a dead end. First doing that
terrible thing and now going where you get boxed in by the river
toward your own coffin. It doesn't make sense for me to follow
you in there. You'll have to come back as soon as you see that
you're hemmed in. I'll wait for you here. I'll use the time to prac-
tice my aim, to plan where I'm going to have the bullet hit you.
I'm patient, and you're not, and that's to my advantage. My heart
is healthy, sliding and turning in its own blood, and yours is worn
out, shriveled and rotting away. That's to my advantage too. You'll
be dead tomorrow, or maybe the day after tomorrow, or in a week.
Time doesn't matter. I'm patient."

The man saw that the river was narrowing between steep cliffs,
and he stopped. *"I'll have to go back,"* he said.

In this area the river is wide and deep and there are no rapids.
It slides into a channel like thick, dirty oil. And now and then it
swallows a branch in its whirlpools, sucking it down without any
noise of protest.

"Son," said the one who was sitting there waiting, "it doesn't
matter if I tell you now that the man who killed you is dead from
this moment on. Will I gain anything from that? The thing is that
I wasn't with you. What's the use of explaining anything? I wasn't

there with you. That's all there is to it. Nor with her. Nor him. I wasn't with anyone, because the newborn baby shut my mind out to everything else."

The man went up the river a long stretch.

Bubbles of blood boiled through his mind. *"I thought the first one was going to wake up the rest with his death rattle, that's why I hurried."* "Excuse my haste," he said to them. And then he felt that the gurgling noise sounded like people snoring; that's why he became so calm when he went outside into the night, into the cold of that cloudy night.

He seemed to be running away. His shanks were so caked with mud that you couldn't tell what the color of his pants was.

I saw him from the moment he dived into the river.

He hunched his body and then he floated downstream without moving his arms, as if he were walking on the bottom. Then he reached the shore and put his clothes out to dry. I saw he was trembling with the cold. It was windy and cloudy.

I was peering through the break in the fence where my boss had me in charge of his sheep. I turned and looked at that man without his suspecting anybody was spying on him.

He moved his arms up and down and stretched and relaxed his body, letting it air out so it would dry. Then he put on his ragged shirt and pants. I saw he didn't have a machete or any weapon. Just the empty holster which hung down from his belt.

He looked and looked in every direction and then he left. And I was just getting ready to go round up my sheep when I saw him come back with the same lost look.

He plunged into the river again, into the middle fork, on the way back.

The man

"What's the matter with this fellow?" I asked myself.

That's all. He faced the current and it whipped him around like a shuttlecock and he almost drowned. He thrashed about with his arms, but he couldn't get across and he came ashore down below, coughing up water until you thought his insides were coming out.

He went through the operation of drying himself out again, all naked, and then he took off back up the river the way he'd come.

I wish I had him here now. If I'd known what he'd done I would've crushed him with stones and I wouldn't even be sorry.

I figured he was running away. You just had to see his face. But, Señor Licenciado, I'm not a mind reader. I'm only a sheepherder and I guess I get kind of scared sometimes. Though, like you say, I could've easily caught him off guard, and a stone well aimed at his head would've left him there stiff as a board. You're right, however you look at it.

After hearing from you about all those murders he committed earlier and just a short time ago I can't forgive myself. I like to kill killers, believe me. It's not what's usually done, but it must feel nice to help God finish off those sons of the devil.

But that isn't the whole story. I saw him come back the next day. But I still didn't know anything. If I had!

I saw him come along skinnier than the day before, with his bones sticking out of his skin and his shirt torn. I didn't think it was him, he looked so different.

I recognized him by the look in his eyes—very hard as if they could hurt you. I saw him take a drink and then fill his mouth with water like he was rinsing it out; but what had happened was that he'd swallowed a good mouthful of mud puppies, because the pool where he drank was shallow and swarming with mud puppies. He must've been hungry.

I looked at his eyes, which were two dark holes like caves.

He came up close to me and said, "Are those your sheep," I told him they weren't. "They belong to their mother," that's what I told him.

He didn't think it was funny. He didn't even laugh. He grabbed the fattest one of my ewes and with his hands like pincers he held her feet and sucked on her teats. You could hear the animal's bleating clear up here; but he didn't let her go, just went on sucking and sucking until he'd got enough. You can imagine what it was like when I tell you I had to put creosote on her udders to take the swelling out and so she wouldn't be infected by the bites he'd taken on her.

You say he killed the whole Urquidi family? If I'd known, I would've kept him from getting away just by beating him with a stick of wood.

But you don't know what's going on when you live way up in the mountains, with just the sheep for company, and sheep don't know any gossip.

The next day he appeared again. When I arrived, he did too. And we even got friendly.

He told me he wasn't from these parts, but from far away; but that he couldn't walk because his legs were giving out on him: "I walk and walk and don't cover any ground. My legs are so weak they buckle on me. And my country is far away, farther than those mountains." He told me he'd gone two days without eating anything except weeds. That's what he told me.

You say he wasn't even sorry when he killed the Urquidi family? If I'd known, he would've been done for right then, with his mouth open while he was drinking my sheep's milk.

But he didn't seem bad. He told me about his wife and kids. And how far away they were from him. He sniffled when he remembered them.

And he was terribly skinny, as thin as a rail. Just yesterday he ate a piece of an animal that had been killed by lightning. One part of the sheep was most likely eaten by the ants and the part that was left he roasted on the coals I'd lit to warm my tortillas and he finished it off. He gnawed the bones clean.

"The poor animal died of sickness," I told him.

But it was just like he didn't hear me. He gobbled it all up. He was hungry.

But you say he murdered those people. If I'd only known. You see what it's like to be ignorant and trusting. I'm just a sheepherder and that's all I know. I don't know what you'll think when I tell you that he ate from my very own tortillas and dipped them in my plate!

So now when I come to tell you what I know, I'm in cahoots with him? That's the way it is. And you say you're going to throw me in jail for hiding that guy? Like I was the one who killed that family. I just came to tell you that there's a dead man in a pool of the river. And you ask me since when and what that man's like and something about him. And now when I tell you, I'm covering up for him. Well, so that's the way it is.

Believe me, Señor Licenciado, if I'd known who that man was I would've found a way to kill him. But what did I know? I'm not a mind reader. All he did was ask me for something to eat and talk to me about his children, with the tears running down his face.

And now he's dead. I thought he'd placed his clothes to dry among the river rocks; but it was him, stretched out face down in the water. First I thought he'd fallen on his face like that when he bent over the river and that he couldn't raise his head and then had started to breathe in water, until I saw the thick blood coming out of his mouth and the back of his neck full of holes as if they'd drilled him. I just came to tell you what happened, without adding anything or leaving anything out. I'm a sheepherder and that's all I know anything about.

$\mathcal{A}t$ daybreak

San Gabriel emerges from the fog laden with dew. The clouds of the night slept over the village searching for the warmth of the people. Now the sun is about to come out and the fog rises slowly, rolling up its sheet, leaving white strips over the roof tops. A gray steam, hardly visible, rises from the trees and the wet earth, attracted by the clouds, but it vanishes immediately. Then the black smoke comes from the kitchens, smelling of burned oak, covering the sky with ashes.

In the distance the mountains are still in shadow.

A swallow swoops across the streets, and then the first peal of dawn rings out.

The lights are turned off. Then an earth-colored spot shrouds the village, which keeps on snoring a little longer, slumbering in the color of daybreak.

Along the Jiquilpan road, bordered by fig trees, comes old Esteban mounted on the back of a cow, driving his milking herd. He

At daybreak

got up there so the grasshoppers wouldn't jump at his face. He scares away the mosquitoes with his hat and now and then tries to whistle at the cows with his toothless mouth so they won't lag behind. They plod along chewing their cuds, splashing themselves with the dew on the grass. It's getting light. He hears the San Gabriel bells that ring at daybreak and gets down off the cow, kneeling on the ground and making the sign of the cross with his arms extended.

An owl hoots in the hollow of the trees, and then Esteban jumps up again on the cow's back, takes off his shirt so the breeze will whip away his fear, and continues on his way.

"One, two . . . ten," he counts the cows as they pass over the cattleguard at the edge of town. He grabs one of them by the ears and says to her, pulling on her face, "Now they're going to take away your baby, you silly one. Carry on if you want to, but it's the last day you'll see your calf." The cow tranquilly gazes at him, switches him with her tail, and walks on.

They're ringing the last bell at daybreak.

It isn't known whether the swallows come from Jiquilpan or San Gabriel; but they swoop, zigzagging back and forth, dipping their breasts in the muddy pools without breaking their flight; some of them carry things in their beaks; they graze the mud with their tail feathers and fly off, away from the road, vanishing in the dark horizon.

The clouds are now over the mountains, so far away that they just seem to be gray bits of plaster on the slopes of those blue hills.

Old Esteban looks at the colors running serpentine through the sky—reds, oranges, yellows. The stars are turning white. The last twinkles go out and the sun bursts forth, making the blades of grass glisten.

At daybreak

"My bare belly was cold from being out in the air. I don't remember why now. I reached the corral gate and they didn't open up for me. The stone I was knocking on the door with broke and nobody came out. Then I thought my boss, Don Justo, had fallen asleep. I didn't say anything to the cows, or explain anything to them; I slipped off so they wouldn't see me or follow me. I looked for a place where the fence was low, and climbed up over it there and jumped down on the other side in among the calves. And I was just lifting up the bar to open the gate when I saw my boss, Don Justo, came out of the attic with the girl Margarita asleep in his arms and cross the corral without seeing me. I hid, plastering myself against the wall, and I'm sure he didn't see me. At least that's what I thought."

Old Esteban let the cows in one by one while he milked them. He left to the last the one without her calf now, who was bellowing like sixty, until out of pure pity he let her in. "For the last time," he told her, "look at him and lick him; look at him like he was going to die. You're ready to calve again and you're still fussing over this big fellow." And to him: "Enjoy them now, for they're no longer yours; you'll find out that this milk is new milk, like for a newborn calf." And he kicked him when he saw him sucking from the four teats. "I'll smash your snout, you son of a gun."

"And I would've broken his nose if the boss, Don Justo, hadn't appeared suddenly and given me a swift kick to calm me down. He gave me such a beating that I was almost out cold among the rocks, my bones crackling with pain they were so battered. All that day, I remember, I felt very weak and unable to move because of the swelling that resulted and the great deal of pain, which I still have.

At daybreak

"What happened next? I didn't know. I didn't work for him any more. Nor anybody else either, because he died that same day. Didn't you know? They came to my house to tell me, while I was lying down on the cot, with my old woman there beside me putting poultices and wet cloths on me. They came to tell me the news. And they said I had killed him—that's what people were saying. Maybe so, but I can't remember. Don't you think that killing somebody would leave a tell-tale sign? It must, especially if it's your boss. But since they have me here in jail, it must mean something, don't you think? But, look, I remember very well up to the moment when I hit the calf and the boss came at me, up to there I remember very well; afterward everything is hazy. I feel like I suddenly went to sleep and when I woke up I was in my cot with the old woman there by my side comforting me because of my aches and pains as if I was a little kid and not this battered old man that I am. I even said to her, 'Shut up now!' I remember very well that's what I said to her; why shouldn't I remember if I'd killed a man? But, still, they say I killed Don Justo. So they say I killed him? They say with a rock, huh? Well, maybe so, because if they'd said it was with a knife they'd be crazy, because I haven't carried a knife since I was a boy, and that's many, many years ago now."

Justo Brambila left his niece Margarita on the bed, taking care to make no noise. In the next room his sister was sleeping, crippled for two years now, motionless, her body like a rag, but always awake. She only slept briefly at dawn; then she slept heavily like the dead.

She would awaken when the sun came out, now. When Justo Brambila left the sleeping body of Margarita on the bed, she was beginning to open her eyes. She heard her daughter's breathing

and asked, "Where were you last night, Margarita?" And before
the yelling started that would end by waking her up, Justo Brambila silently left the room.

It was six o'clock in the morning.

He went out to the corral to open the gate for old Esteban. He
also thought about going up to the attic to smooth over the bed
where he and Margarita had spent the night. "If the priest would
authorize this I'd marry her; but I'm sure he'll raise an awful fuss
if I ask him. He'll say it's incest and will excommunicate us both.
Better to leave things in secret." That's what he was thinking about
when he found old Esteban struggling with the calf, sticking his
wiry hands in the animal's nose and kicking it in the head. It
seemed like the calf's back already was broken, because it was
flopping its legs on the ground without being able to get up.

He ran and grabbed the old man by the neck and threw him
down against the rocks, kicking him and shouting things at him
that he didn't even know he was capable of saying. Then he felt
himself blacking out and falling back against the stone paving of
the corral. He tried to get up and fell back again, and the third
time he lay still. A huge black cloud covered his sight when he
tried to open his eyes. He didn't feel any pain, just a black thing
that was dimming his thought until the obscurity became total.

Old Esteban got up when the sun was already high. He stumbled
along, moaning. They didn't know how he managed to open the
gate and set out on the street. They didn't know how he got home,
his eyes closed shut, leaving that trickle of blood all along the way.
He got there and lay down on his cot and fell asleep again.

It must have been eleven in the morning when Margarita entered the corral looking for Justo Brambila, crying because her

mother, after a lot of scolding and lecturing, had said she was a prostitute.

She found Justo Brambila dead.

"Well, they say I killed him. Maybe so. But he might've died from anger too. He was very bad-tempered. Everything seemed bad to him: the mangers were dirty, the water troughs didn't have water in them, the cows were very skinny. Everything made him angry; he didn't even like it that I was skinny. And how could I not be skinny when I hardly eat anything. Why, I spent all my time out driving the cows: I took them to Jiquilpan, where he'd bought some pasture; I waited until they'd eaten and then I brought them back by daybreak. It was just one eternal pilgrimage.

"And now see what's happened—they've got me in jail and they're going to judge me next week because I killed Don Justo. I don't remember it, but maybe it happened. Maybe we were both blinded and didn't realize we were killing each other. It could well be. Memory, at my age, is tricky; that's why I thank God that I won't lose much now if they finish off all my faculties, for I hardly have any left. And as for my soul, well, I'll commend it to Him too."

Over San Gabriel the fog was coming in again. The sun still was shining on the blue hills. A brownish spot covered the village. Then darkness came. That night they didn't turn on the lights, in mourning, for Don Justo was the owner of the lights. The dogs howled until dawn. The stained glass in the church was lit up with candlelight until dawn, while they held the wake over the dead man's body. Women sang with falsetto voices in the half-dream of the night: "Come out, come out, come out, souls in torment." And the church bells were ringing for the dead all night, until dawn, until they were cut short by the peals of dawn.

Talpa

Natalia threw herself into her mother's arms, crying on and on with a quiet sobbing. She'd bottled it up for many days, until we got back to Zenzontla today and she saw her mother and began feeling like she needed consolation.

But during those days when we had so many difficult things to do—when we had to bury Tanilo in a grave at Talpa without anyone to help us, when she and I, just the two of us alone, joined forces and began to dig the grave, pulling out the clods of earth with our hands, hurrying to hide Tanilo in the grave so he wouldn't keep on scaring people with his smell so full of death—then she didn't cry.

Not afterward either, on the way back, when we were traveling at night without getting any rest, groping our way as if asleep and trudging along the steps that seemed like blows on Tanilo's grave.

Talpa

At that time Natalia seemed to have hardened and steeled her heart so she wouldn't feel it boiling inside her. Not a single tear did she shed.

She came here, near her mother, to cry, just to upset her, so she'd know she was suffering, upsetting all the rest of us besides. I felt that weeping of hers inside me too as if she was wringing out the cloth of our sins.

Because what happened is that Natalia and I killed Tanilo Santos between the two of us. We got him to go with us to Talpa so he'd die. And he died. We knew he couldn't stand all that traveling; but just the same, we pushed him along between us, thinking we'd finished him off forever. That's what we did.

The idea of going to Talpa came from my brother Tanilo. It was his idea before anyone else's. For years he'd been asking us to take him. For years. From the day when he woke up with some purple blisters scattered about on his arms and legs. And later on the blisters became wounds that didn't bleed—just a yellow gummy thing like thick distilled water came out of them. From that time I remember very well he told us how afraid he was that there was no cure for him any more. That's why he wanted to go see the Virgin of Talpa, so she'd cure him with her look. Although he knew Talpa was far away and we'd have to walk a lot under the sun in the daytime and in the cold March nights, he wanted to go anyway. The blessed Virgin would give him the cure to get rid of that stuff that never dried up. She knew how to do that, by washing them, making everything fresh and new like a recently rained-on field. Once he was there before Her, his troubles would be over; nothing would hurt him then or hurt him ever again. That's what he thought.

And that's what Natalia and I latched on to so we could take him. I had to go with Tanilo because he was my brother. Natalia would have to go too, of course, because she was his wife. She had to help him, taking him by the arm, bearing his weight on her shoulders on the trip there and perhaps on the way back, while he dragged along on his hope.

I already knew what Natalia was feeling inside. I knew something about her. I knew, for example, that her round legs, firm and hot like stones in the noonday sun, had been alone for a long time. I knew that. We'd been together many times, but always Tanilo's shadow separated us; we felt that his scabby hands got between us and took Natalia away so she'd go on taking care of him. And that's the way it'd be as long as he was alive.

I know now that Natalia is sorry for what happened. And I am too; but that won't save us from feeling guilty or give us any peace ever again. It won't make us feel any better to know that Tanilo would've died anyway because his time was coming, and that it hadn't done any good to go to Talpa, so far away, for it's almost sure he would've died just as well here as there, maybe a little afterward, because of all he suffered on the road, and the blood he lost besides, and the anger and everything—all those things together were what killed him off quicker. What's bad about it is that Natalia and I pushed him when he didn't want to go on anymore, when he felt it was useless to go on and he asked us to take him back. We jerked him up from the ground so he'd keep on walking, telling him we couldn't go back now.

"Talpa is closer now than Zenzontla." That's what we told him. But Talpa was still far away then, many days away.

We wanted him to die. It's no exaggeration to say that's what

Talpa

we wanted before we left Zenzontla and each night that we spent on the road to Talpa. It's something we can't understand now, but it was what we wanted. I remember very well.

I remember those nights very well. First we had some light from a wood fire. Afterward we'd let the fire die down, then Natalia and I would search out the shadows to hide from the light of the sky, taking shelter in the loneliness of the countryside, away from Tanilo's eyes, and we disappeared into the night. And that loneliness pushed us toward each other, thrusting Natalia's body into my arms, giving her a release. She felt as if she was resting; she forgot many things and then she'd go to sleep with her body feeling a great relief.

It always happened that the ground on which we slept was hot. And Natalia's flesh, the flesh of my brother Tanilo's wife, immediately became hot with the heat of the earth. Then those two heats burned together and made one wake up from one's dreams. Then my hands groped for her; they ran over her red-hot body, first lightly, but then they tightened on her as if they wanted to squeeze her blood out. This happened again and again, night after night, until dawn came and the cold wind put out the fire of our bodies. That's what Natalia and I did along the roadside to Talpa when we took Tanilo so the Virgin would relieve his suffering.

Now it's all over. Even from the pain of living Tanilo found relief. He won't talk any more about how hard it was for him to keep on living, with his body poisoned like it was, full of rotting water inside that came out in each crack of his legs or arms. Wounds this big, that opened up slow, real slow, and then let out bubbles of stinking air that had us all scared.

But now that he's dead things are different. Now Natalia weeps for him, maybe so he'll see, from where he is, how full of remorse her soul is. She says she's seen Tanilo's face these last days. It was the only part of him that she cared about—Tanilo's face, always wet with the sweat which the effort to bear his pain left him in. She felt it approaching her mouth, hiding in her hair, begging her, in a voice she could scarcely hear, to help him. She says he told her that he was finally cured, that he no longer had any pain. "Now I can be with you, Natalia. Help me to be with you," she says he said to her.

We'd just left Talpa, just left him buried there deep down in that ditch we dug to bury him.

Since then Natalia has forgotten about me. I know how her eyes used to shine like pools lit up by the moon. But suddenly they faded, that look of hers was wiped away as if it'd been stamped into the earth. And she didn't seem to see anything any more. All that existed for her was her Tanilo, whom she'd taken care of while he was alive and had buried when his time came to die.

It took us twenty days to get to the main road to Talpa. Up to then the three of us had been alone. At that point people coming from all over began to join us, people like us who turned onto that wide road, like the current of a river, making us fall behind, pushed from all sides as if we were tied to them by threads of dust. Because from the ground a white dust rose up with the swarm of people like corn fuzz that swirled up high and then came down again; all the feet scuffling against it made it rise again, so that dust was above and below us all the time. And above this land was the empty sky, without any clouds, just the dust, and the dust didn't give any shade.

We had to wait until nighttime to rest from the sun and that white light from the road.

Talpa

Then the days began to get longer. We'd left Zenzontla about the middle of February, and now that we were in the first part of March it got light very early. We hardly got our eyes closed at night when the sun woke us up again, the same sun that'd gone down just a little while ago.

I'd never felt life so slow and violent as when we were trudging along with so many people, just like we were a swarm of worms all balled together under the sun, wriggling through the cloud of dust that closed us all in on the same path and had us corralled. Our eyes followed the dust cloud and struck the dust as if stumbling against something they could not pass through. And the sky was always gray, like a heavy gray spot crushing us all from above. Only at times, when we crossed a river, did the dust clear up a bit. We'd plunge our feverish and blackened heads into the green water, and for a moment a blue smoke, like the steam that comes out of your mouth when it's cold, would come from all of us. But a little while afterward we'd disappear again, mixed in with the dust, sheltering each other from the sun, from that heat of the sun we all had to endure.

Eventually night will come. That's what we thought about. Night will come and we'll get some rest. Now we have to get through the day, get through it somehow to escape from the heat and the sun. Then we'll stop—afterward. What we've got to do now is keep plugging right along behind so many others just like us and in front of many others. That's what we have to do. We'll really only rest well when we're dead.

That's what Natalia and I thought about, and maybe Tanilo too, when we were walking along the main road to Talpa among the procession, wanting to be the first to reach the Virgin, before she ran out of miracles.

But Tanilo began to get worse. The time came when he didn't want to go any farther. The flesh on his feet had burst open and begun to bleed. We took care of him until he got better. But, he'd decided not to go any farther.

"I'll sit here for a day or two and then I'll go back to Zenzontla." That's what he said to us.

But Natalia and I didn't want him to. Something inside us wouldn't let us feel any pity for Tanilo. We wanted to get to Talpa with him, for at that point he still had life left in him. That's why Natalia encouraged him while she rubbed his feet with alcohol so the swelling would go down. She told him that only the Virgin of Talpa would cure him. She was the only one who could make him well forever. She and no one else. There were lots of other Virgins, but none like the Virgin of Talpa. That's what Natalia told him.

Then Tanilo began to cry, and his tears made streaks down his sweaty face, and he cursed himself for having been bad. Natalia wiped away the streaky tears with her shawl, and between us we lifted him off the ground so he'd walk on a little further before night fell.

So, dragging him along was how we got to Talpa with him.

The last few days we started getting tired too. Natalia and I felt that our bodies were being bent double. It was as if something was holding us and placing a heavy load on top of us. Tanilo fell down more often and we had to pick him up and sometimes carry him on our backs. Maybe that's why we felt the way we did, with our bodies slack and with no desire to keep on walking. But the people who were going along by us made us walk faster.

At night that frantic world calmed down. Scattered everywhere the bonfires shone, and around the fire the pilgrims said their rosaries, with their arms crossed, gazing toward the sky in the direction of Talpa. And you could hear how the wind picked up and carried that noise, mixing it together until it was all one roaring sound. A little bit afterward everything would get quiet. About midnight you could hear someone singing far away. Then you closed your eyes and waited for the dawn to come without getting any sleep.

We entered Talpa singing the hymn praising Our Lord.

We'd left around the middle of February and we got to Talpa the last days of March, when a lot of people were already on their way back. All because Tanilo took it into his head to do penance. As soon as he saw himself surrounded by men wearing cactus leaves hanging down like scapularies, he decided to do something like that too. He tied his feet together with his shirt sleeves so his steps became more desperate. Then he wanted to wear a crown of thorns. A little later he bandaged his eyes, and still later, during the last part of the way, he knelt on the ground and shuffled along on his knees with his hands crossed behind him; so that thing that was my brother Tanilo Santos reached Talpa, that thing so covered with plasters and dried streaks of blood that it left in the air a sour smell like a dead animal when he passed by.

When we least expected it we saw him there among the dancers. We hardly realized it and there he was with a long rattle in his hand, stomping hard on the ground with his bare bruised feet. He seemed to be in a fury, as if he was shaking out all the anger he'd been carrying inside him for such a long time, or making a last effort to try to live a little longer.

Maybe when he saw the dances he remembered going every year to Tolimán during the novena of Our Lord and dancing all night long until his bones limbered up without getting tired. Maybe that's what he remembered and he wanted to get back the strength he used to have.

Natalia and I saw him like that for a moment. Right afterward we saw him raise his arms and slump to the ground with the rattle still sounding in his bloodspecked hands. We dragged him out so he wouldn't be tromped on by the dancers, away from the fury of those feet that slipped on stones and leaped about stomping the earth without knowing that something had fallen among them.

Holding him up between us as if he was crippled, we went into the church with him. Natalia had him kneel down next to her before that little golden figure of the Virgin of Talpa. And Tanilo started to pray and let a huge tear fall, from way down inside him, snuffing out the candle Natalia had placed in his hands. But he didn't realize this; the light from so many lit candles kept him from realizing what was happening right there. He went on praying with his candle snuffed out. Shouting his prayers so he could hear himself praying.

But it didn't do him any good. He died just the same.

"... from our hearts filled with pain we all send her the same plea. Many laments mixed with hope. Her tenderness is not deaf to laments nor tears, for She suffers with us. She knows how to take away that stain and to leave the heart soft and pure to receive her mercy and charity. Our Virgin, our mother, who wants to know nothing of our sins, who blames herself for our sins, who wanted to bear us in her arms so life wouldn't hurt us, is right here by us, relieving our tiredness and the sicknesses of our souls and our bodies filled with thorns, wounded and supplicant. She knows that each day our faith is greater because it is made up of sacrifices ..."

That's what the priest said from up in the pulpit. And after he quit talking the people started praying all at once with a noise just like a lot of wasps frightened by smoke.

But Tanilo no longer heard what the priest was saying. He'd become still, with his head resting on his knees. And when Natalia moved him so he'd get up he was already dead.

Outside you could hear the noise of the dancing, the drums and the hornpipes, the ringing of bells. That's when I got sad. To see so many living things, to see the Virgin there, right in front of us with a smile on her face, and to see Tanilo on the other hand as if he was in the way. It made me sad.

But we took him there so he'd die, and that's what I can't forget.

Now the two of us are in Zenzontla. We've come back without him. And Natalia's mother hasn't asked me anything, what I did with my brother Tanilo, or anything. Natalia started crying on her shoulder and poured out the whole story to her.

I'm beginning to feel as if we hadn't reached any place; that we're only here in passing, just to rest, and that then we'll keep on traveling. I don't know where to, but we'll have to go on, because here we're very close to our guilt and the memory of Tanilo.

Maybe until we begin to be afraid of each other. Not saying anything to each other since we left Talpa may mean that. Maybe Tanilo's body is too close to us, the way it was stretched out on the rolled petate, filled inside and out with a swarm of blue flies that buzzed like a big snore coming from his mouth, that mouth we couldn't shut in spite of everything we did and that seemed to want to go on breathing without finding any breath. That Tanilo, who didn't feel pain any more but who looked like he was still in pain with his hands and feet twisted and his eyes wide open like he was looking at his own death. And here and there all his wounds dripping a yellow water, full of that smell that spread everywhere and that you could taste in your mouth, like it was a thick and bitter honey melting into your blood with each mouthful of air you took.

I guess that's what we remember here most often—that Tanilo we buried in the Talpa graveyard, that Tanilo Natalia and I threw earth and stones on so the wild animals wouldn't come dig him up.

The burning Plain

They've gone and killed the bitch
but the puppies still remain . . .
(Popular Ballad)

V iva Petronilo Flores!"

The cry echoed along the walls of the barranca and rose up to where we were. Then it faded.

For a while the wind blowing from below brought us a tumult of voices scrambled together, making a noise just like rising water when it rolls over stony stretches. Then, coming from the same place, another cry twisted up from the bend of the barranca, re-echoed along the walls, and reached us still strong: "Viva mi General Petronilo Flores!"

We looked at each other.

La Perra got up slowly, took out the cartridge from his gun and put it in his shirt pocket. Then he came up to where Los Cuatro were and said to them, "Follow me, boys, and we'll see what bulls we're going to fight." The four Benavides brothers walked behind him, stooped over; only La Perra marched along very stiff and straight, half of his thin body appearing above the fence.

We stayed there, motionless. We were lined up at the foot of the

The burning Plain

fence, stretched out on our backs, like iguanas warming themselves in the sun.

The stone fence snaked about climbing up and down the hills, and La Perra and the four Benevides also snaked along as if their feet were tied. That's the way they looked when we lost sight of them. Then we turned our faces again to look up, looking at the low chinaberry branches that shaded us a bit.

That's the way it smelled—shade warmed over by the sun. Rotten chinaberries.

We felt the noonday drowsiness.

The racket from down below came up out of the barranca at short intervals and shook our bodies so we couldn't sleep. And though we tried to listen, cocking our ears carefully, all we could make out was that racket, ripples of noise, like listening to the sound ox carts make on a rocky street.

Suddenly a shot rang out. The barranca, repeating the noise, sounded like it was being torn apart. The noise made things wake up: the totochilos, those red birds we'd been watching play among the chinaberries, and the locusts that'd gone to sleep in the noonday heat woke up, filling the earth with their shrill cries.

"What was that?" asked Pedro Zamora, still half groggy from his siesta.

Then El Chihuila got up, and dragging his gun like it was a piece of firewood set out behind those who'd gone.

"I'm going to see what it was," he said, passing out of sight like the others.

The chirping of the locusts increased until it was deafening, and we didn't realize when they appeared there. When we least expected it, here they were already, right in front of us, and all unprepared. They seemed to be just passing by, not at all equipped for this encounter.

We turned and looked at them through our gun sights.

The first group passed, then the second, and still more, their bodies bent forward, hunched over with sleepiness. Their faces shone with sweat, as if they had dived into the water on crossing the arroyo.

They kept on passing by.

The signal came. There was a long whistle, and the yak-yak of rifles began from far off, where La Perra had gone. Then it continued here.

It was easy. They almost closed the gun-sight holes with their bulk, so that it was like shooting them at close range and knocking them over like ninepins without their hardly realizing it.

But this lasted just a little while—maybe the first and second rounds of fire. Soon, peering through the gun-sight holes, we saw only those who were lying in the middle of the road, half twisted, as if someone had come along and thrown them there. Then they appeared again, then suddenly they weren't there any more.

For the next round of fire we had to wait.

One of our men shouted, "Viva Pedro Zamora!"

From the other side they answered, almost whispering, "Save me, boss! Save me! Holy Child of Atocha, help me!"

Birds flew by. Flocks of thrushes crossed above us headed for the hills.

The third round of shots came from behind us. It spurted from them, making us jump to the other side of the fence, beyond the men we'd killed.

Then we started running, taking cover among the thickets. We

The burning Plain

felt the bullets cracking at our heels, and it felt like we'd fallen on a swarm of grasshoppers. And from time to time, and more and more often, the bullets were striking right among us, knocking over one of us with a crunch of bones.

We ran. We reached the edge of the barranca and let ourselves slide down it pell-mell.

They were still firing. They kept on firing until we'd climbed up the other side on all fours, like badgers scared by the light.

"Viva General Petronilo Flores, you sons of bitches!" they yelled at us again. And the cry went rebounding like a thunderstorm down the barranca.

We remained crouched down behind some big round stones, still breathing heavily from our running. We just looked at Pedro Zamora, asking him with our eyes what had happened to us. But he returned our looks without saying anything. It was as if our speech had run out or our tongues had gotten balled up like parrots' do and we had a very hard time untangling them in order to say anything.

Pedro Zamora was still looking at us. He was counting with his eyes, those eyes of his, all red, as if he never slept. He counted us one by one. He knew now how many of us were there, but he seemed not to be quite sure yet; that's why he counted us over and over again.

Some were missing—eleven or twelve, without counting La Perra and El Chihuila and the others who'd gone with them. El Chihuila might well be crouched up high in some chinaberry tree, resting against the butt of his gun, waiting for the federal forces to leave.

The burning Plain

Los Joseses, La Perra's two sons, were the first to raise their heads, then their bodies. Finally they walked from one side to another, waiting for Pedro Zamora to tell them something. And he said, "Another slaughter like this one and we're done for."

Then right away, choked up as if swallowing a mouthful of anger, he shouted at Los Joseses, "I know your father is missing, but hold on, hold on a bit! We'll go after him!"

A bullet shot from over yonder made a flock of kildees fly up on the opposite side. The birds swooped over the barranca and fluttered about quite near us, then when they saw us, got frightened, gave a half wheel, glittering against the sun, and again filled the trees on the other side with their cries.

Los Joseses returned to their previous place and squatted down in silence.

There we stayed all afternoon. When night began to fall El Chihuila arrived accompanied by one of Los Cuatro. They told us they came from down below, from Piedra Lisa, but they couldn't tell us whether the Federals had withdrawn. Everything certainly seemed to be calm. From time to time you could hear the coyotes howling.

"Hey, Pichón!" Pedro Zamora said to me. "I'm going to give you a commission to go with Los Joseses to Piedra Lisa and see what happened to La Perra. If he's dead, well, bury him. And do the same with the others. Leave the wounded up on something so the soldiers will see them, but don't bring anybody back."

"We'll do it."

And we went.

You could hear the coyotes closer when we reached the corral where we'd left the horses. There weren't any horses left, just a skinny burro that lived there before we'd come. Of course, the Federals had taken our horses.

We found the rest of Los Cuatro behind some bushes, the three of them together, one piled on top of another as if they'd been stacked up there. We raised their heads and shook them a little to see if they gave any signs of life, but no, they were stone dead. In the watering trough was another one of our men with his ribs sticking out, as if he'd been hacked with a machete. Scouting all along the fence from top to bottom we came across one here and another there, almost all with blackened faces.

"They really killed these; no hope for them," said one of Los Joseses.

We started looking for La Perra, not paying attention to any of the rest, just trying to find the famous Perra. We didn't find him.

"They must've taken him with them," we thought. "They must've taken him to show him to the government." But even so, we continued looking everywhere among the stubble. The coyotes kept on howling.

They kept on howling all night long.

A few days later at El Armería where you cross the river we met Petronilo Flores. We turned back but it was too late. It was as if they'd shot us. Pedro Zamora took the lead, spurring to a gallop his roan mule that was the best animal I ever knew. And behind him, in a drove we came, bent over our horses' necks. The slaughter was terrific. I didn't realize it right away because I sank down in the river under my dead horse, and the current dragged us both a long way to a shallow pool of water filled with sand.

That was the last time we fought with Petronilo Flores' troops. After that we quit fighting. Or you might say, we passed some time without fighting, trying to keep ourselves hidden; that's why the few of us that were left decided to take to the woods, going up in the hills to hide from the persecution. And we ended up being such small scattered groups that nobody was afraid of us any more. Nobody ran shouting now, "Here come Zamora's men!"

Peace had returned to the Great Plain.

But not for long.

About eight months we'd been hiding in a secret place in Tozín Canyon, where the Armería River is boxed in the canyon for many hours before falling swiftly down to the coast. We hoped to let some years go by before returning to the world, when nobody would remember us any more. We'd started to raise chickens and now and then we climbed up in the mountains hunting for deer. There were five of us, more like four, because one of Los Joseses got gangrene in his leg just below the buttock from a bullet, when they were firing at us from the rear.

There we were, beginning to feel we were no longer good for anything. And if we hadn't known they'd hang us all, we'd have gone asking for peace.

But at that moment a certain Armancio Alcalá, who delivered messages and letters for Pedro Zamora, appeared.

It was early in the morning, while we were busy cutting up a cow we'd slaughtered, when we heard the whistle. It came from far off in the direction of the Plain. A little later we heard it again. It was like a bull's bellow: first sharp, then hoarse, then sharp again. The echo stretched it out until it came close to us, until the murmuring of the river drowned it out. And the sun was about to come out when Alcalá himself appeared among some cypress trees. He was carrying over his shoulder two cartridge belts with forty-four cartridges, and across his horse's haunches a mountain of rifles were slung like a suitcase.

The burning Plain

He dismounted. He gave us each a rifle and then rearranged the bundle with the rifles that were left.

"If you have nothing urgent to do today and tomorrow, get ready to leave for San Buenaventura. Pedro Zamora will be waiting for you there. Meanwhile, I'm going a little further downhill to look for Los Zanates. Then I'll come back."

The next day he came back late in the afternoon. And yes, Los Zanates were with him. You could make out their black faces in the dusk of the afternoon. Three others were coming with them that we didn't know.

"We'll get horses on the way," they told us. And we followed them.

Long before reaching San Buenaventura we realized that the ranch buildings were on fire. From the hacienda's barns the flames rose highest, and it looked like a pool of oil was being burned up. The sparks flew and spiraled in the darkness of the sky, forming great lit-up clouds.

We kept marching ahead, inflamed by the blaze from San Buenaventura, as if something told us that our job was there, to finish off what remained.

But we hadn't managed to get there when we met the first ones on horseback, coming at a trot, their ropes tied to the front of their saddles, some of them pulling men who'd been shot and were still able to walk on their hands part of the time, and others pulling men whose hands had now fallen and whose heads hung down.

We watched them go by. Further behind came Pedro Zamora and a lot of men on horseback. More men than ever before. It pleased us.

We were pleased to see that long file of men crossing the Big Plain again, like in the good old days, like in the beginning when we'd risen up from the earth like ripe burrs fanned by the wind to fill all that region of the Plain with terror. For a time that's the way it was. And now it seemed like it was returning.

From there we struck off toward San Pedro. We set fire to it and then we set out for Petacal. It was just about time for the corn to be harvested and the cornfields were dry and bent over by the strong winds that blow on the Plain in this season. So it was very nice to see the fire march along through the pastures, to see almost the whole Plain become a burning coal in that bonfire, with the smoke weaving up above, that smoke that smelled of cane and honey because the fire had reached the canefields too.

We came out of the smoke like scarecrows, with our faces smudgy, driving cattle here and there to get them together in some place and skin them. That was our business—cowhides.

Because as Pedro Zamora said to us, "We're going to have this revolution with the money of the rich. They'll pay for the arms and the expenses this revolution costs. And even if we don't have any flag right now to fight for, we must hurry and pile up money, so when the government troops come they'll see that we're powerful." That's what he said.

And when the troops came at last, they let loose killing us again, as they did before, but not as easily. Now it was clear from leagues away that they were afraid of us.

But we were afraid of them too. It was a sight to see how our balls slid up to our throats just hearing the noise their harness made or the clicking of their horses' hooves on the stones of some road when we were waiting for them in ambush. As we watched them go by we almost felt like they were looking sidewise at us and saying, "We've sniffed you out, we're just pretending, that's all."

The burning Plain

That's the way it seemed to be too, because suddenly they'd throw themselves on the ground, fortified behind their horses, and they'd hold us off there, until some others encircled us little by little, catching us there like trapped chickens. That's when we knew we weren't going to last very long, even if there were a lot of us.

The reason is that it wasn't General Urbano's men any more, who'd been sent against us in the beginning and who got scared just from a little shouting and hat waving, those men recruited by force from their ranches so they'd fight us and who'd only dare attack when they saw there weren't very many of us. There weren't any more of them. Others took their place later, and these were the worst. A certain Olachea led them now, and his men were brave and could stand a lot, highland men brought from Teocaltiche, mixed with Tepehuan Indians from the north—Indians with heavy heads of hair, used to going without food for many days and who sometimes waited for hours spying on you with their eyes fixed, without blinking, waiting for you to show your head so they could shoot, straight at you, one of those long-distance, thirty-thirty bullets that broke your spine like it was breaking a rotten branch.

Why should we go on this way, when it was easier to swoop down on the ranches instead of ambushing the federal troops. That's why we scattered, and with a little strike here and another there we did more damage than ever, always on the run, shooting and running like crazy mules.

And so, while some of us were setting fire to the Jazmín ranches on the slopes of the volcano, others suddenly descended on military detachments, dragging along huizache branches and making them think there were a whole bunch of us, hidden among the dust clouds and the cries we made.

The burning Plain

The soldiers had no choice but to wait there. For a while they ran from one side to another, back and forth, like crazy. From here you could see the bonfires on the mountain, huge fires as if they were burning the clearings. From here we watched the ranches and small villages burning day and night, and sometimes bigger towns like Tuzamilpa and Zapotitlán, that lit up the sky. And then Olachea's men would strike out for those places on forced marches, but when they got there, Totolimispa, way over this way behind them, would start to burn.

That was a fine sight to see. To come out suddenly from a thicket of mezquite trees when the soldiers, itching to fight, had gone, and see them cross the empty plain, no enemy in sight, as if they were diving into the deep bottomless water of that great horseshoe plain ringed by mountains.

We burned El Cuastecomate and we played bullfighting there. Pedro Zamora liked this game a lot.

The federal troops had gone in the direction of Autlán, looking for a place called La Purificación, where they thought the bandits' hideout we'd come from was. They went and left us alone at El Cuastecomate.

There we had a chance to play bullfighting. They'd left eight soldiers they'd forgotten about, besides the administrator and foreman of the hacienda. We had two days of bullfighting.

We had to make a little round corral like those they use to pen up goats to serve as the bull ring. And we sat on the fence so the bullfighters couldn't get out, for they ran real hard as soon as they saw the razor Pedro Zamora wanted to gore them with.

The eight soldiers were good for one afternoon. The other two

for the other. And the one who gave the most trouble was that foreman, long and skinny like a bamboo pole, who got out of the way
just by slipping sideways a little. On the other hand, the administrator died right off. He was real short and pot-bellied and he didn't
try any tricks to dodge the razor. He died very quietly, almost without moving and as if he himself had wished to be stabbed. But the
foreman sure caused trouble.

Pedro Zamora had loaned each one of them a blanket, and that's
the reason why at least the foreman defended himself so well from
the razor stabs with that heavy thick blanket; for as soon as he
found out what to expect, he shook the blanket against the razor
which came straight at him, and he kept on dodging in this way
until Pedro Zamora got tired of it. You could see real clear how
tired he was of charging the foreman, without being able to give
him anything except a few grazing nicks, and he lost his patience.
But he kept on with the same tactics for a while, until suddenly,
instead of charging straight ahead the way bulls do, he went for
the foreman's ribs with his razor, while he shoved the blanket aside
with his other hand. The foreman didn't seem to realize what had
happened, because he kept on waving the blanket up and down
for a good while as if he was scaring off wasps. He only stopped
moving when he saw his blood running down his waist. He got
frightened and with his fingers tried to stop up the hole in his side
where that red stuff which made him get real pale came out in a
solid stream. Then he collapsed in the middle of the corral, staring
up at all of us. And he stayed there until we strung him up, because otherwise he would've taken a long time to die.

Since then Pedro Zamora played the bull right along, whenever
he got a chance to.

During those times we were almost all from the lowlands, from

Pedro Zamora on down; later, people from other parts joined us—light-skinned Indians from Zacoalco, tall and long-legged, with cottage-cheese faces, and those others from the cold highlands called Mazamitla, who always wore sarapes as if it was snowing all the time. They lost their appetite with the heat, and that's the reason Pedro Zamora sent them to guard the Pass of the Volcanoes, way up high where there was just sand and rocks washed by the wind. But the light-skinned Indians soon took a fancy to Pedro Zamora and didn't want to leave him. They were always right there at his heels, protecting him and carrying out all the orders he wanted them to do. Sometimes they even carried off the best girls in the towns so he could have them.

I remember it all very well. The nights we spent on the mountain, marching without making any noise and real sleepy when the troops were already close behind us. I still see Pedro Zamora with his purple-red blanket rolled up on his shoulders, watching out that nobody strayed behind: "Come on, Pitasio, spur that horse! And don't you go to sleep on me, Reséndiz, because I need you to talk to!"

Yes, he watched out for us. We marched along right through the middle of the night with our eyes dazed with sleep and without a thought in our heads; but he knew all of us and kept talking to us so we wouldn't fall asleep. We felt those eyes of his wide open, those eyes that didn't sleep and were used to seeing at night and recognizing us in the dark. He'd count us, one by one, like counting money. Then he'd come up to our side. We'd hear his horse's hooves and we'd know that his eyes were always on the alert. That's why all of us, without complaining about how cold and sleepy we were, followed him quietly as if we were blind.

But everything broke down completely after the train derailment

The burning Plain

on the Sayula hill. If that hadn't happened maybe Pedro Zamora would still be alive, and El Chino Arias and El Chihuila and so many others, and the revolution would have gone on its merry way. But Pedro Zamora got the government's goat with the train derailment at Sayula.

I can still see the glare from the flames that rose where they piled up the dead. They shoveled them together or made them roll like tree trunks down the hill, and when the pile got big they drenched it with gas and set fire to it. The stink was carried far off by the wind and many days later you could still smell scorched flesh.

A little before that we hadn't really known what was going to happen. We'd spread cow bones and horns along a long stretch of the track, and as if this wasn't enough, we'd bent the rails apart where the train would start around a curve. We did that and waited.

Dawn was beginning to light things up. You could almost clearly make out the people crowded together on the roof of the cars. You could hear some of them singing. Men's and women's voices. They passed in front of us still half in the shadow of the night, but we could see that they were soldiers with their women. We waited. The train didn't stop.

If we'd wanted to, we could've sniped at the train, because it was moving slow and puffing, as if it was trying to climb up the hill by pure grunting. We could even have conversed with them a bit. But things turned out differently.

They started to realize what was happening to them when they felt the cars swerve and the train sway like somebody was shaking it. Then the locomotive backed down, dragged from the track by the heavy cars filled with people. It let out some hoarse, sad, real long whistles. But nobody helped it. It kept sliding back, dragged by that train you couldn't see the end of, until there wasn't any level ground under it, and tipping over on its side, it plunged to the bottom of the barranca. Then the cars followed it, one after another, lickety-split, each one tumbling down to its place below. Afterward, everything was still, as if everybody, even us, had died.

That's the way it happened.

When the survivors started crawling out through the splintered cars, we got away from there, cramped with fear.

We stayed in hiding several days, but the federal troops came to flush us out. They didn't leave us alone any more, not even to munch on a piece of jerky. They saw to it that we didn't have time to eat or sleep, and the days and nights all became one to us. We tried to reach Tozín Canyon, but the government forces got there ahead of us. We skirted the volcano. We climbed the highest mountains, and at that place called El Camino de Dios we found the government troops again shooting to kill. We felt the bullets pepper us, heating the air all around us. And even the rocks we hid behind were shattered one after another as if they were clods of earth. Later we found out those arms they were shooting at us with were machine guns that left your body like a sieve, but at the time we thought there were just a lot of soldiers, thousands of them, and all we wanted to do was get away from them.

Those of us who could got away. El Chihuila stayed there at El Camino de Dios, slumped down behind a madrone tree with his blanket wrapped around his neck like he was defending himself from the cold. He lay there looking at us as each of us left, sharing his death with us. And he seemed to be laughing at us, with his bared teeth, stained red with blood.

The way we scattered turned out all right for many of us, but for some it was bad. It was unusual if we didn't see one of our men strung up by the feet on just any tree along the roads. They stayed there too until they got old and curled up like untanned hides. The buzzards ate their insides, gutting them, until they left just the shell. And since they were strung up high, they stayed there rustling in the breeze for many days, sometimes months, sometimes nothing more than just strips of pants moving in the wind, as if somebody had hung them out to dry there. And you felt like things were really getting serious when you saw that.

Some of us made it to the Big Hill and creeping along like snakes we spent our time looking toward the Plain, toward that land down below where we were born and had lived and where they were waiting now to kill us. Sometimes even the shadow of the clouds scared us.

We'd have been glad to go tell somebody we were no longer fighting men and to leave us in peace, but because we'd done so much damage on one side and another, the people had turned against us and all we had managed to make were enemies. Even the Indians up here didn't like us any more. They said we'd killed off their animals. And now they go around with arms the government gave them and they've sent us word they'll kill us if they see us: "We don't want to see you, but if we do, we'll kill you" was what they said.

So there was hardly any place on earth left for us to go. We hardly had a bit of ground left to be buried in. That's the reason why the last of us decided to separate, each one going in a different direction.

I was with Pedro Zamora about five years. Good days, bad days, they came to five years. I never saw him after that. They say he went to Mexico City running after a woman and that he was killed there. Some of us were waiting for him to come back, but we got tired of waiting. He still hasn't come back. He was killed there. A man who was in jail with me told me about their killing him.

I got out of jail three years ago. They punished me there for a lot of crimes, but not because I was one of Zamora's men. They didn't know that. They got me for other things, among others for the bad habit I had of carrying off girls. Now one of them is living with me, maybe the finest and best woman in the world—the one who was there, outside the jail waiting I don't know how long for them to let me loose.

"Pichón, I'm waiting for you," she said to me. "I've been waiting for you for a long time."

I figured then that she was waiting to kill me. Dimly, like it was a dream, I remembered who she was. I felt again the cold water of the storm falling that night we entered Telcampana and plundered the town. I was almost sure her father was that old man we sent to his resting place as we were leaving, shot in the head by one of us while I yanked his daughter up over the saddle of my horse and gave her a few whacks so she'd calm down and quit biting me. She was a young girl about fourteen with pretty eyes and she put up a lot of fight; it was a real job taming her.

"I have a son of yours," she said to me then. "There he is."

And she pointed with her finger at a tall skinny boy with frightened eyes: "Take off your hat so your father can see you!"

And the boy took off his hat. He was just like me and with something mean in his look. He had to get some of that from his father.

"They call him 'El Pichón' too," the woman, who is now my wife, went on saying. "But he's not a bandit or a killer. He's a good person."

I hung my head.

Tell them not to kill me!

Tell them not to kill me, Justino! Go on and tell them that. For God's sake! Tell them. Tell them please for God's sake."

"I can't. There's a sergeant there who doesn't want to hear anything about you."

"Make him listen to you. Use your wits and tell him that scaring me has been enough. Tell him please for God's sake."

"But it's not just to scare you. It seems they really mean to kill you. And I don't want to go back there."

"Go on once more. Just once, to see what you can do."

"No. I don't feel like going. Because if I do they'll know I'm your son. If I keep bothering them they'll end up knowing who I am and will decide to shoot me too. Better leave things the way they are now."

Tell them not to kill me!

"Go on, Justino. Tell them to take a little pity on me. Just tell them that."

Justino clenched his teeth and shook his head saying no.

And he kept on shaking his head for some time.

"Tell the sergeant to let you see the colonel. And tell him how old I am— How little I'm worth. What will he get out of killing me? Nothing. After all he must have a soul. Tell him to do it for the blessed salvation of his soul."

Justino got up from the pile of stones which he was sitting on and walked to the gate of the corral. Then he turned around to say, "All right, I'll go. But if they decide to shoot me too, who'll take care of my wife and kids?"

"Providence will take care of them, Justino. You go there now and see what you can do for me. That's what matters."

They'd brought him in at dawn. The morning was well along now and he was still there, tied to a post, waiting. He couldn't keep still. He'd tried to sleep for a while to calm down, but he couldn't. He wasn't hungry either. All he wanted was to live. Now that he knew they were really going to kill him, all he could feel was his great desire to stay alive, like a recently resuscitated man.

Who would've thought that old business that happened so long ago and that was buried the way he thought it was would turn up? That business when he had to kill Don Lupe. Not for nothing either, as the Alimas tried to make out, but because he had his reasons. He remembered: Don Lupe Terreros, the owner of the Puerta de Piedra—and besides that, his compadre—was the one he, Juvencio Nava, had to kill, because he'd refused to let him pasture his animals, when he was the owner of the Puerta de Piedra and his compadre too.

Tell them not to kill me!

At first he didn't do anything because he felt compromised. But later, when the drouth came, when he saw how his animals were dying off one by one, plagued by hunger, and how his compadre Lupe continued to refuse to let him use his pastures, then was when he began breaking through the fence and driving his herd of skinny animals to the pasture where they could get their fill of grass. And Don Lupe didn't like it and ordered the fence mended, so that he, Juvencio Nava, had to cut open the hole again. So, during the day the hole was stopped up and at night it was opened again, while the stock stayed there right next to the fence, always waiting—his stock that before had lived just smelling the grass without being able to taste it.

And he and Don Lupe argued again and again without coming to any agreement.

Until one day Don Lupe said to him, "Look here, Juvencio, if you let another animal in my pasture, I'll kill it."

And he answered him, "Look here, Don Lupe, it's not my fault that the animals look out for themselves. They're innocent. You'll have to pay for it, if you kill them."

And he killed one of my yearlings.

This happened thirty-five years ago in March, because in April I was already up in the mountains, running away from the summons. The ten cows I gave the judge didn't do me any good, or the lien on my house either, to pay for getting me out of jail. Still later they used up what was left to pay so they wouldn't keep after me, but they kept after me just the same. That's why I came to live with my son on this other piece of land of mine which is called Palo de Venado. And my son grew up and got married to my daughter-in-law Ignacia and has had eight children now. So it happened a long time ago and ought to be forgotten by now. But I guess it's not.

85

Tell them not to kill me!

I figured then that with about a hundred pesos everything could be fixed up. The dead Don Lupe left just his wife and two little kids still crawling. And his widow died soon afterward too—they say from grief. They took the kids far off to some relatives. So there was nothing to fear from them.

But the rest of the people took the position that I was still summoned to be tried just to scare me so they could keep on robbing me. Every time someone came to the village they told me, "There are some strangers in town, Juvencio."

And I would take off to the mountains, hiding among the madrone thickets and passing the days with nothing to eat but herbs. Sometimes I had to go out at midnight, as though the dogs were after me. It's been that way my whole life. Not just a year or two. My whole life.

And now they've come for him when he no longer expected anyone, confident that people had forgotten all about it, believing that he'd spend at least his last days peacefully. "At least," he thought, "I'll have some peace in my old age. They'll leave me alone."

He'd clung to this hope with all his heart. That's why it was hard for him to imagine that he'd die like this, suddenly, at this time of life, after having fought so much to ward off death, after having spent his best years running from one place to another because of the alarms, now when his body had become all dried up and leathery from the bad days when he had to be in hiding from everybody.

Hadn't he even let his wife go off and leave him? The day when he learned his wife had left him, the idea of going out in search of her didn't even cross his mind. He let her go without trying to find out at all who she went with or where, so he wouldn't have to go down to the village. He let her go as he'd let everything else go, without putting up a fight. All he had left to take care of was his life, and he'd do that, if nothing else. He couldn't let them kill him. He couldn't. Much less now.

But that's why they brought him from there, from Palo de Venado. They didn't need to tie him so he'd follow them. He walked alone, tied by his fear. They realized he couldn't run with his old body, with those skinny legs of his like dry bark, cramped up with the fear of dying. Because that's where he was headed. For death. They told him so.

That's when he knew. He began to feel that stinging in his stomach that always came on suddenly when he saw death nearby, making his eyes big with fear and his mouth swell up with those mouthfuls of sour water he had to swallow unwillingly. And that thing that made his feet heavy while his head felt soft and his heart pounded with all its force against his ribs. No, he couldn't get used to the idea that they were going to kill him.

There must be some hope. Somewhere there must still be some hope left. Maybe they'd made a mistake. Perhaps they were looking for another Juvencio Nava and not him.

He walked along in silence between those men, with his arms fallen at his sides. The early morning hour was dark, starless. The wind blew slowly, whipping the dry earth back and forth, which was filled with that odor like urine that dusty roads have.

His eyes, that had become squinty with the years, were looking down at the ground, here under his feet, in spite of the darkness. There in the earth was his whole life. Sixty years of living on it, of holding it tight in his hands, of tasting it like one tastes the flavor of meat. For a long time he'd been crumbling it with his eyes, savoring each piece as if it were the last one, almost knowing it would be the last.

Then, as if wanting to say something, he looked at the men who

87

Tell them not to kill me!

were marching along next to him. He was going to tell them to let him loose, to let him go; "I haven't hurt anybody, boys," he was going to say to them, but he kept silent. "A little further on I'll tell them," he thought. And he just looked at them. He could even imagine they were his friends, but he didn't want to. They weren't. He didn't know who they were. He watched them moving at his side and bending down from time to time to see where the road continued.

He'd seen them for the first time at nightfall, that dusky hour when everything seems scorched. They'd crossed the furrows trodding on the tender corn. And he'd gone down on account of that—to tell them that the corn was beginning to grow there. But that didn't stop them.

He'd seen them in time. He'd always had the luck to see everything in time. He could've hidden, gone up in the mountains for a few hours until they left and then come down again. Already it was time for the rains to have come, but the rains didn't come and the corn was beginning to wither. Soon it'd be all dried up.

So it hadn't even been worthwhile, his coming down and placing himself among those men like in a hole, never to get out again.

And now he continued beside them, holding back how he wanted to tell them to let him go. He didn't see their faces, he only saw their bodies, which swung toward him and then away from him. So when he started talking he didn't know if they'd heard him. He said, "I've never hurt anybody." That's what he said. But nothing changed. Not one of the bodies seemed to pay attention. The faces didn't turn to look at him. They kept right on, as if they were walking in their sleep.

Then he thought that there was nothing else he could say, that he would have to look for hope somewhere else. He let his arms fall again to his sides and went by the first houses of the village, among those four men, darkened by the black color of the night.

"Colonel, here is the man."

They'd stopped in front of the narrow doorway. He stood with his hat in his hand, respectfully, waiting to see someone come out. But only the voice came out, "Which man?"

"From Palo de Venado, colonel. The one you ordered us to bring in."

"Ask him if he ever lived in Alima," came the voice from inside again.

"Hey, you. Ever lived in Alima?" the sergeant facing him repeated the question.

"Yes. Tell the colonel that's where I'm from. And that I lived there till not long ago."

"Ask him if he knew Guadalupe Terreros."

"He says did you know Guadalupe Terreros?"

"Don Lupe? Yes. Tell him that I knew him. He's dead."

Then the voice inside changed tone: "I know he died," it said. And the voice continued talking, as if it was conversing with someone there on the other side of the reed wall.

"Guadalupe Terreros was my father. When I grew up and looked for him they told me he was dead. It's hard to grow up knowing that the thing we have to hang on to to take roots from is dead. That's what happened to us.

"Later on I learned that he was killed by being hacked first with a machete and then an ox goad stuck in his belly. They told me he lasted more than two days and that when they found him, lying in an arroyo, he was still in agony and begging that his family be taken care of.

Tell them not to kill me!

"As time goes by you seem to forget this. You try to forget it. What you can't forget is finding out that the one who did it is still alive, feeding his rotten soul with the illusion of eternal life. I couldn't forgive that man, even though I don't know him; but the fact that I know where he is makes me want to finish him off. I can't forgive his still living. He should never have been born."

From here, from outside, all he said was clearly heard. Then he ordered, "Take him and tie him up awhile, so he'll suffer, and then shoot him!"

"Look at me, colonel!" he begged. "I'm not worth anything now. It won't be long before I die all by myself, crippled by old age. Don't kill me!"

"Take him away!" repeated the voice from inside.

"I've already paid, colonel. I've paid many times over. They took everything away from me. They punished me in many ways. I've spent about forty years hiding like a leper, always with the fear they'd kill me at any moment. I don't deserve to die like this, colonel. Let the Lord pardon me, at least. Don't kill me! Tell them not to kill me!"

There he was, as if they'd beaten him, waving his hat against the ground. Shouting.

Immediately the voice from inside said, "Tie him up and give him something to drink until he gets drunk so the shots won't hurt him."

Finally, now, he'd been quieted. There he was, slumped down at the foot of the post. His son Justino had come and his son Justino had gone and had returned and now was coming again.

He slung him on top of the burro. He cinched him up tight against the saddle so he wouldn't fall off on the road. He put his

90

head in a sack so it wouldn't give such a bad impression. And then he made the burro giddap, and away they went in a hurry to reach Palo de Venado in time to arrange the wake for the dead man.

"Your daughter-in-law and grandchildren will miss you," he was saying to him. "They'll look at your face and won't believe it's you. They'll think the coyote has been eating on you when they see your face full of holes from all those bullets they shot at you."

ℒuvina

Of the mountains in the south Luvina is the highest and the rockiest. It's infested with that gray stone they make lime from, but in Luvina they don't make lime from it or get any good out of it. They call it crude stone there, and the hill that climbs up toward Luvina they call the Crude Stone Hill. The sun and the air have taken it on themselves to make it crumble away, so that the earth around there is always white and brilliant, as if it were always sparkling with the morning dew, though this is just pure talk, because in Luvina the days are cold as the nights and the dew thickens in the sky before it can fall to the earth.

And the ground is steep and slashed on all sides by deep barrancas, so deep you can't make out the bottom. They say in Luvina that one's dreams come up from those barrancas; but the only thing I've seen come up out of them was the wind, whistling as if down below they had squeezed it into reed pipes. A wind that doesn't even let the dulcamaras grow: those sad little plants that can live with just a bit of earth, clutching with all their hands at the mountain cliffsides. Only once in a while, where there's a little shade, hidden among the rocks, the chicalote blossoms with its white poppies. But the chicalote soon withers. Then you hear it scratching the air with its spiny branches, making a noise like a knife on a whetstone.

"You'll be seeing that wind that blows over Luvina. It's dark. They say because it's full of volcano sand; anyway, it's a black air. You'll see it. It takes hold of things in Luvina as if it was going to bite them. And there are lots of days when it takes the roofs off the houses as if they were hats, leaving the bare walls uncovered. Then it scratches like it had nails: you hear it morning and night, hour after hour without stopping, scraping the walls, tearing off strips of earth, digging with its sharp shovel under the doors, until you feel it boiling inside of you as if it was going to remove the hinges of your very bones. You'll see."

The man speaking was quiet for a bit, while he looked outside.

The noise of the river reached them, passing its swollen waters through the fig-tree branches, the noise of the air gently rustling the leaves of the almond trees, and the shouts of the children playing in the small space illumined by the light that came from the store.

The flying ants entered and collided with the oil lamp, falling to the ground with scorched wings. And outside night kept on advancing.

"Hey, Camilo, two more beers!" the man said again. Then he added, "There's another thing, mister. You'll never see a blue sky in Luvina. The whole horizon there is always a dingy color, always clouded over by a dark stain that never goes away. All the hills are bare and treeless, without one green thing to rest your eyes on; everything is wrapped in an ashy smog. You'll see what it's like—those hills silent as if they were dead and Luvina crowning the highest hill with its white houses like a crown of the dead—"

The children's shouts came closer until they penetrated the store. That made the man get up, go to the door and yell at them, "Go away! Don't bother us! Keep on playing, but without so much racket."

Then, coming back to the table, he sat down and said, "Well, as I was saying, it doesn't rain much there. In the middle of the year they get a few storms that whip the earth and tear it away, just leaving nothing but the rocks floating above the stony crust. It's good to see then how the clouds crawl heavily about, how they march from one hill to another jumping as if they were inflated bladders, crashing and thundering just as if they were breaking on the edge of the barrancas. But after ten or twelve days they go away and don't come back until the next year, and sometimes they don't come back for several years— No, it doesn't rain much. Hardly at all, so that the earth, besides being all dried up and shriveled like old leather, gets filled with cracks and hard clods of earth like sharp stones, that prick your feet as you walk along, as if the earth itself had grown thorns there. That's what it's like."

He downed his beer, until only bubbles of foam remained in the bottle, then he went on: "Wherever you look in Luvina, it's a very sad place. You're going there, so you'll find out. I would say it's the place where sadness nests. Where smiles are unknown as if people's faces had been frozen. And, if you like, you can see that sadness just any time. The breeze that blows there moves it around but never takes it away. It seems like it was born there. And you can almost taste and feel it, because it's always over you, against you, and because it's heavy like a large plaster weighing on the living flesh of the heart.

Luvina

"The people from there say that when the moon is full they clearly see the figure of the wind sweeping along Luvina's streets, bearing behind it a black blanket; but what I always managed to see when there was a moon in Luvina was the image of despair— always.

"But drink up your beer. I see you haven't even tasted it. Go ahead and drink. Or maybe you don't like it warm like that. But that's the only kind we have here. I know it tastes bad, something like burro's piss. Here you get used to it. I swear that there you won't even get this. When you go to Luvina you'll miss it. There all you can drink is a liquor they make from a plant called hojasé, and after the first swallows your head'll be whirling around like crazy, feeling like you had banged it against something. So better drink your beer. I know what I'm talking about."

You could still hear the struggle of the river from outside. The noise of the air. The children playing. It seemed to be still early in the evening.

The man had gone once more to the door and then returned, saying: "It's easy to see things, brought back by memory, from here where there's nothing like it. But when it's about Luvina I don't have any trouble going right on talking to you about what I know. I lived there. I left my life there— I went to that place full of illusions and returned old and worn out. And now you're going there— All right. I seem to remember the beginning. I'll put myself in your place and think— Look, when I got to Luvina the first time— But will you let me have a drink of your beer first? I see you aren't paying any attention to it. And it helps me a lot. It relieves me, makes me feel like my head had been rubbed with camphor oil— Well, I was telling you that when I reached Luvina the first time, the mule driver who took us didn't even want to let his animals rest. As soon as he let us off, he turned half around. 'I'm going back,' he said.

" 'Wait, aren't you going to let your animals take a rest? They are all worn out.'

" 'They'd be in worse shape here,' he said. 'I'd better go back.'

"And away he went, rushing down Crude Stone Hill, spurring his horses on as if he was leaving some place haunted by the devil.

"My wife, my three children, and I stayed there, standing in the middle of the plaza, with all our belongings in our arms. In the middle of that place where all you could hear was the wind—

"Just a plaza, without a single plant to hold back the wind. There we were.

"Then I asked my wife, 'What country are we in, Agripina?'

"And she shrugged her shoulders.

" 'Well, if you don't care, go look for a place where we can eat and spend the night. We'll wait for you here,' I told her.

"She took the youngest child by the hand and left. But she didn't come back.

"At nightfall, when the sun was lighting up just the tops of the mountains, we went to look for her. We walked along Luvina's narrow streets, until we found her in the church, seated right in the middle of that lonely church, with the child asleep between her legs.

" 'What are you doing here, Agripina?'

" 'I came in to pray,' she told us.

" 'Why?' I asked her.

"She shrugged her shoulders.

"Nobody was there to pray to. It was a vacant old shack without any doors, just some open galleries and a roof full of cracks where the air came through like a sieve.

" 'Where's the restaurant?'

" 'There isn't any restaurant.'

" 'And the inn?'

" 'There isn't any inn.'

" 'Did you see anybody? Does anybody live here?' I asked her.

" 'Yes, there across the street— Some women— I can still see them. Look, there behind the cracks in that door I see some eyes shining, watching us— They have been looking over here— Look at them. I see the shining balls of their eyes— But they don't have anything to give us to eat. They told me without sticking out their heads that there was nothing to eat in this town— Then I came in here to pray, to ask God to help us.'

" 'Why didn't you go back to the plaza? We were waiting for you.'

" 'I came in here to pray. I haven't finished yet.'

" 'What country is this, Agripina?'

"And she shrugged her shoulders again.

"That night we settled down to sleep in a corner of the church behind the dismantled altar. Even there the wind reached, but it wasn't quite as strong. We listened to it passing over us with long howls, we listened to it come in and out of the hollow caves of the doors whipping the crosses of the stations of the cross with its hands full of air—large rough crosses of mesquite wood hanging from the walls the length of the church, tied together with wires that twanged with each gust of wind like the gnashing of teeth.

"The children cried because they were too scared to sleep. And my wife, trying to hold all of them in her arms. Embracing her handful of children. And me, I didn't know what to do.

"A little before dawn the wind calmed down. Then it returned. But there was a moment during that morning when everything was still, as if the sky had joined the earth, crushing all noise with its weight— You could hear the breathing of the children, who now were resting. I listened to my wife's heavy breath there at my side.

" 'What is it?' she said to me.

" 'What's what?' I asked her.

" 'That, that noise.'

" 'It's the silence. Go to sleep. Rest a little bit anyway, because it's going to be day soon.'

"But soon I heard it too. It was like bats flitting through the darkness very close to us. Bats with big wings that grazed against the ground. I got up and the beating of wings was stronger, as if the flock of bats had been frightened and were flying toward the holes of the doors. Then I walked on tiptoes over there, feeling that dull murmur in front of me. I stopped at the door and saw them. I saw all the women of Luvina with their water jugs on their shoulders, their shawls hanging from their heads and their black figures in the black background of the night.

" 'What do you want?' I asked them. 'What are you looking for at this time of night?'

"One of them answered, 'We're going for water.'

"I saw them standing in front of me, looking at me. Then, as if they were shadows, they started walking down the street with their black water jugs.

"No, I'll never forget that first night I spent in Luvina.

"Don't you think this deserves another drink? Even if it's just to take away the bad taste of my memories."

"It seems to me you asked me how many years I was in Luvina, didn't you? The truth is, I don't know. I lost the notion of time since the fevers got it all mixed up for me, but it must have been an eternity— Time is very long there. Nobody counts the hours and nobody cares how the years go mounting up. The days begin and end. Then night comes. Just day and night until the day of death, which for them is a hope.

"You must think I'm harping on the same idea. And I am, yes, mister— To be sitting at the threshold of the door, watching the rising and the setting of the sun, raising and lowering your head, until the springs go slack and then everything gets still, timeless, as if you had always lived in eternity. That's what the old folks do there.

"Because only real old folks and those who aren't born yet, as they say, live in Luvina— And weak women, so thin they are just skin and bones. The children born there have all gone away— They hardly see the light of day and they're already grown up. As they say, they jump from their mothers' breasts to the hoe and disappear from Luvina. That's the way it is in Luvina.

"There are just old folks left there and lone women, or with a husband who is off God knows where— They appear every now and then when the storms come I was telling you about; you hear a rustling all through the town when they return and something like a grumbling when they go away again— They leave a sack of provisions for the old folks and plant another child in the bellies of their women, and nobody knows anything more of them until the next year, and sometimes never— It's the custom. There they think that's the way the law is, but it's all the same. The children spend their lives working for their parents as their parents worked for theirs and who knows how many generations back performed this obligation—

"Meanwhile, the old people wait for them and for death, seated in their doorways, their arms hanging slack, moved only by the gratitude of their children— Alone, in that lonely Luvina.

"One day I tried to convince them they should go to another place where the land was good. 'Let's leave here!' I said to them. 'We'll manage somehow to settle somewhere. The government will help us.'

"They listened to me without batting an eyelash, gazing at me from the depths of their eyes from which only a little light came.

" 'You say the government will help us, teacher? Do you know the government?'

"I told them I did.

" 'We know it too. It just happens. But we don't know anything about the government's mother.'

"I told them it was their country. They shook their heads saying no. And they laughed. It was the only time I saw the people of Luvina laugh. They grinned with their toothless mouths and told me no, that the government didn't have a mother.

"And they're right, you know? That lord only remembers them when one of his boys has done something wrong down here. Then he sends to Luvina for him and they kill him. Aside from that, they don't know if the people exist.

" 'You're trying to tell us that we should leave Luvina because you think we've had enough of going hungry without reason,' they said to me. 'But if we leave, who'll bring along our dead ones? They live here and we can't leave them alone.'

"So they're still there. You'll see them now that you're going. Munching on dry mesquite pulp and swallowing their own saliva to keep hunger away. You'll see them pass by like shadows, hugging to the walls of the houses, almost dragged along by the wind.

" 'Don't you hear that wind?' I finally said to them. 'It will finish you off.'

" 'It keeps on blowing as long as it ought to. It's God's will,' they answered me. 'It's bad when it stops blowing. When that happens the sun pours into Luvina and sucks our blood and the little bit of moisture we have in our skin. The wind keeps the sun up above. It's better that way.'

"So I didn't say anything else to them. I left Luvina and I haven't gone back and I don't intend to.

"—But look at the way the world keeps turning. You're going there now in a few hours. Maybe it's been fifteen years since they said the same thing to me: 'You're going to San Juan Luvina.'

"In those days I was strong. I was full of ideas— You know how we're all full of ideas. And one goes with the idea of making something of them everywhere. But it didn't work out in Luvina. I made the experiment and it failed—

"San Juan Luvina. That name sounded to me like a name in the heavens. But it's purgatory. A dying place where even the dogs have died off, so there's not a creature to bark at the silence; for as soon as you get used to the strong wind that blows there all you hear is the silence that reigns in these lonely parts. And that gets you down. Just look at me. What it did to me. You're going there, so you'll soon understand what I mean—

"What do you say we ask this fellow to pour a little mescal? With this beer you have to get up and go all the time and that interrupts our talk a lot. Hey, Camilo, let's have two mescals this time!

"Well, now, as I was telling you—"

But he didn't say anything. He kept staring at a fixed point on the table where the flying ants, now wingless, circled about like naked worms.

Outside you could hear the night advancing. The lap of the water against the fig-tree trunks. The children's shouting, now far away. The stars peering through the small hole of the door.

The man who was staring at the flying ants slumped over the table and fell asleep.

The night they left him alone

Why are you going so slow?" Feliciano Ruelas asked those ahead of him. "We'll end up falling asleep this way. Don't you have the urge to get there soon?"

"We'll get there tomorrow at dawn," they answered him.

It was the last thing he heard them say. Their last words. But he would only remember that afterward, the next day.

The three of them went along, their eyes on the ground, trying to take advantage of the little bit of brightness in the night.

"Better that it's dark. That way they won't see us." They'd said that too, a little earlier, or perhaps last night. He didn't remember. The ground clouded his thoughts.

Now, climbing, he saw the ground again. He felt it coming toward him, surrounding him, trying to find the place where he was the tiredest, until it was above him, over his back, where his rifles were slung.

Where the terrain was level he walked fast. When the uphill part began, he got behind; his head started to nod, slower and slower,

The night they left him alone

as his steps shortened. The others passed him by; now they were far ahead, and he followed, nodding his sleepy head.

He was getting way behind. The road lay before him, almost at eye level. And the weight of the rifles. And sleep overtaking him in the curve of his back.

He heard the footsteps dying away—those hollow clicks made by the heels he'd been listening to for God knows how long, during God knows how many nights. "From La Magdalena to here, the first night; then from here to there, the second; and this is the third. It wouldn't be so many nights," he thought, "if only we'd slept during the day. But they didn't want to. 'They might catch us asleep,' they said. 'And that would be the worst that could happen'."

"The worst for whom?"

Now he was talking in his sleep. "I told them to wait: let's leave this day for rest. Tomorrow we'll march in a file and feel more like it, with more strength if we have to run. We might have to."

He stopped with his eyes closed. "It's too much," he said. "What do we gain by hurrying? Just one day. After losing so many, it isn't worth it." Immediately afterward he shouted, "Where are you now?"

And almost to himself, "Well, go on then, go on!"

He leaned back against a tree trunk. The ground was cold and his sweat turned to cold water. This must be the mountains they'd talked to him about. Down there the warm land, and now up here this cold that got in under his overcoat, "as if they had lifted up my shirt and run their icy hands over my skin."

He sank down on the moss. He opened his arms as if he wanted to take the measure of the night. He breathed an air that smelled of turpentine. Then he let himself slip into sleep on the cochal plant, feeling his body get stiff with the cold.

The night they left him alone

The cold of dawn woke him up—the wetness of the dew.

He opened his eyes. He saw transparent stars in a clear sky above the dark branches.

"It's getting dark," he thought. And he went back to sleep.

He got up when he heard shouts and the rapid click of hooves on the dry pavement of the road. A yellow light bordered the horizon.

The mule drivers passed by, looking at him. They greeted him, "Good morning!" But he didn't answer.

He remembered what he had to do. It was day now, and he should've crossed the mountains at night to avoid the sentries. This was the safest pass. They'd told him so.

He picked up his guns and slung them over his shoulder. He turned off the road and cut over the mountain toward where the sun was rising. He climbed up and down, crossing clumps of hills.

He seemed to hear the mule drivers saying, "We saw him up there. This is what he looks like, and he's carrying lots of arms."

He threw away the rifles. Then he got rid of the cartridge belts. He felt much lighter and he began to run as if he wanted to beat the mule drivers down the hill.

One had to "climb up, go around the plateau and then down." That's what he was doing. God's will be done. He was doing what they told him to, but not during the hours they told him.

He reached the edge of the deep canyons. He saw the great gray plain far in the distance.

"They must be there. Resting in the sun, without any worry now," he thought.

And he let himself roll down the canyon—rolling, then running, then rolling again.

"God's will be done," he said. And down he rolled faster and faster.

The night they left him alone

He kept hearing the mule drivers when they said to him, "Good morning!" He sensed that their eyes were deceitful. They'll reach the first sentry and say to him, "We saw him in such and such a place. It won't take long for him to get here."

Suddenly he was quiet.

"Christ!" he said. And he was about to shout, "Long live Christ, Our Lord!" but he restrained himself. He took his pistol out of the holster and thrust it inside his shirt to feel it near his flesh. That gave him courage. He approached the houses at Agua Zarca with quiet steps, watching the noisy movements of the soldiers who were warming themselves near large bonfires.

He reached the fence of the corral and could see them better and recognize their faces; they were his uncles Tanis and Librado. While the soldiers moved about around the fire, they were swinging, hanging from a mesquite in the middle of the camp. They no longer seemed to be bothered by the smoke rising from the bonfires which clouded their glassy eyes and blackened their faces.

He tried not to keep looking at them. He dragged himself along the fence and crouched down in a corner, resting his body, though he felt that a worm was twisting about in his stomach.

Above him he heard somebody say, "What are we waiting for to take them down?"

"We're waiting for the other one to come. They say there were three of them, so there must be three. They say the third one is just a boy, but all the same, he was the one who laid the ambush for Lieutenant Parra and wiped out his men. He'll have to come this way like the others did who were older and more experienced. My major says that if he doesn't come today or tomorrow, we'll finish off the first one who passes by and so our orders will be carried out."

The night they left him alone

"And wouldn't it be better if we went out to look for him? That way we wouldn't be so bored either."

"We don't need to. He's got to come this way. They're all bound for the sierra of Comanja to join the conservative forces of the Catorce. These are the last of them. It'd be a good idea to let them pass so they could battle with our companions in the mountains."

"That'd be good. If that happens maybe they'll send us there too."

Feliciano Ruelas waited awhile until the butterflies he felt in his stomach calmed down. Then he took a gulp of air as if he were going to dive into the water, and, flattening himself, crept along the ground by pushing his body with his hands.

When he reached the edge of the arroyo he raised his head and then began to run, opening his path through the tall grass. He didn't look back or stop running until he felt the arroyo dissolve into the plain.

Then he stopped. He breathed deeply, in trembling gulps.

Remember

Remember Urbano Gómez, Don Urbano's son, Dimas' grandson, the one who directed the shepherd's songs and who died reciting the "cursed angel growls" during the influenza epidemic. That was a long time ago, maybe fifteen years. But you ought to remember him. Remember we called him "Grandfather" because his other son, Fidencio Gómez, had two very frisky daughters, one dark and short who'd been given the mean nickname of "Stuck Up," and the other who was real tall and had blue eyes— and they even said she wasn't his—and, if you want any further description, she suffered from hiccups. Remember the commotion she caused when we were in Mass and at the very moment of the Elevation she had an attack of hiccups—it seemed like she was laughing and crying at the same time—until they took her outside and gave her a little water with sugar and then she calmed down. She wound up marrying Lucio Chico, the owner of the tavern

Remember

that used to belong to Librado, up the river, where the Teódulos' linseed mill is.

Remember they called his mother the "Eggplant" because she was always getting into trouble and every time she ended up with a child. They say she had a bit of money, but she used it all up in the burials, because all her children died soon after they were born and she always had masses sung for them, bearing them to the graveyard with music, and a choir of boys who sang "hosannas" and "glories" and that song that goes "Here I send thee, Lord, another little angel." That's how she got to be poor—each funeral cost her a lot because of the drinks she served the guests at the wake. Only two of them lived, Urbano and Natalia, who were born poor, and she didn't see them grow up because she died in her last childbirth, when she was getting along in years, close to fifty.

You must've known her, for she was a scrapper, always getting into arguments with the women selling at the market; when they wanted to charge her too much for tomatoes, she'd raise a ruckus and say they were robbing her. Later, when she was poor, you'd see her scrounging around in the garbage, gathering together scraps of onions and stewed beans and now and then a piece of sugar cane "to sweeten the mouths of her children." She had two, like I told you, that were the only ones who survived. Later, nothing more was known about her.

That Urbano Gómez was more or less our age—maybe a few months older—very good at pitching pennies and cheating in games. Remember he sold us pinks and we'd buy them from him when the easiest thing to do was go out and pick them on the mountain. He sold us green mangoes he stole from the mango tree in the school patio and oranges with chile that he bought at the school gate for two cents and then resold to us for five. He raffled off all the junk he carried in his pockets: agate marbles, tops and spinners, and even green beetles, that kind you tie a thread to their legs so they won't fly very far away. He got the best of all of us, remember.

He was Nachito Rivero's brother-in-law, that Nachito who shortly after he married got feeble-minded, and his wife, Inés, to support herself, had to set up a fruit-drink stand out on the highway, while Nachito spent the day playing songs that were all out of tune on a mandolin they loaned him in Don Refugio's barber shop.

And we'd go with Urbano to see his sister, and to drink the fruit juice we always owed her for and never paid for, because we never had any money. Later on he didn't have any friends left, because all of us, when we'd see him, would avoid him so he wouldn't collect from us.

Maybe that's when he turned bad, or maybe he was just that way right from birth.

They expelled him from school before the fifth year, because he was found with his cousin Stuck Up down in a dry well playing man and wife behind the lavatories. They yanked him by the ears out the main door while everybody laughed like sixty, passing him between a row of boys and girls to make him feel ashamed of himself. And he marched along there with his face held high, shaking his fist at all of us, like he was saying, "You'll pay plenty for this."

And then her. She came out with her face all puckered up and her eyes down on the brick floor until she burst into tears at the door, a shrill weeping you could hear all afternoon like it was a coyote's howl.

Only if your memory's real bad you won't remember that.

Remember

They say his uncle Fidencio, the one at the mill, gave him such a beating it almost left him paralyzed, and he got so mad he left the village.

What we know for sure is we didn't see him again around here till he came back turned into a policeman. He'd always be in the main square, seated on a bench with his gun between his legs and staring at all of us filled with hate. He didn't talk to anybody. He didn't say hello to anybody. And if anybody looked at him, he pretended he didn't know you.

That was when he killed his brother-in-law, the one with the mandolin. Nachito decided to go to serenade him when it was already night, a little after eight o'clock, when they still were ringing the bells for the souls in purgatory. Then there were screams and the people in the church saying their rosaries ran out and saw them there: Nachito on his back defending himself with the mandolin and Urbano hitting him again and again with the butt of his mauser, not hearing what the people shouted at him, rabid, like a sick dog. Until somebody who wasn't even from here came out of the crowd and went up and took the gun away from him and hit him on the back with it, collapsing him over the garden bench where he lay stretched out.

They let him spend the night there. When it was daylight he left. They say that first he went to the parish and he even asked the priest's blessing, but he didn't give it to him.

They arrested him on the road. He was limping and while he sat down to rest they caught up with him. He didn't put up any opposition. They say that he himself tied the rope around his neck and even picked out the tree of his choice for them to hang him from.

You must remember him, because we were classmates at school, and you knew him just like I did.

No dogs bark

You up there, Ignacio! Don't you hear something or see a light somewhere?"

"I can't see a thing."

"We ought to be near now."

"Yes, but I can't hear a thing."

"Look hard. Poor Ignacio."

The long black shadow of the men kept moving up and down, climbing over rocks, diminishing and increasing as it advanced along the edge of the arroyo. It was a single reeling shadow.

The moon came out of the earth like a round flare.

"We should be getting to that town, Ignacio. Your ears are uncovered, so try to see if you can't hear dogs barking. Remember they told us Tonaya was right behind the mountain. And we left the mountain hours ago. Remember, Ignacio?"

"Yes, but I don't see a sign of anything."

"I'm getting tired."

No dogs bark

"Put me down."

The old man backed up to a thick wall and shifted his load but didn't let it down from his shoulders. Though his legs were buckling on him, he didn't want to sit down, because then he would be unable to lift his son's body, which they had helped to sling on his back hours ago. He had carried him all this way.

"How do you feel?"

"Bad."

Ignacio didn't talk much. Less and less all the time. Now and then he seemed to sleep. At times he seemed to be cold. He trembled. When the trembling seized him, his feet dug into his father's flanks like spurs. Then his hands, clasped around his father's neck, clutched at the head and shook it as if it were a rattle.

The father gritted his teeth so he wouldn't bite his tongue, and when the shaking was over he asked, "Does it hurt a lot?"

"Some," Ignacio answered.

First Ignacio had said, "Put me down here— Leave me here— You go on alone. I'll catch up with you tomorrow, or as soon as I get a little better." He'd said this some fifty times. Now he didn't say it.

There was the moon. Facing them. A large red moon that filled their eyes with light and stretched and darkened its shadow over the earth.

"I can't see where I'm going any more," the father said.

No answer.

The son up there was illumined by the moon. His face, discolored, bloodless, reflected the opaque light. And he here below.

"Did you hear me, Ignacio? I tell you I can't see you very well."

No answer.

Falteringly, the father continued. He hunched his body over, then straightened up to stumble on again.

116

"This is no road. They told us Tonaya was behind the hill. We've passed the hill. And you can't see Tonaya, or hear any sound that would tell us it is close. Why won't you tell me what you see up there, Ignacio?"

"Put me down, Father."

"Do you feel bad?"

"Yes."

"I'll get you to Tonaya. There I'll find somebody to take care of you. They say there's a doctor in the town. I'll take you to him. I've already carried you for hours, and I'm not going to leave you lying here now for somebody to finish off."

He staggered a little. He took two or three steps to the side, then straightened up again.

"I'll get you to Tonaya."

"Let me down."

His voice was faint, scarcely a murmur. "I want to sleep a little."

"Sleep up there. After all, I've got a good hold on you."

The moon was rising, almost blue, in a clear sky. Now the old man's face, drenched with sweat, was flooded with light. He lowered his eyes so he wouldn't have to look straight ahead, since he couldn't bend his head, tightly gripped in his son's hands.

"I'm not doing all this for you. I'm doing it for your dead mother. Because you were her son. That's why I'm doing it. She would've haunted me if I'd left you lying where I found you and hadn't picked you up and carried you to be cured as I'm doing. She's the one who gives me courage, not you. From the first you've caused me nothing but trouble, humiliation, and shame."

He sweated as he talked. But the night wind dried his sweat. And over the dry sweat, he sweated again.

"I'll break my back, but I'll get to Tonaya with you, so they can ease those wounds you got. I'm sure as soon as you feel well you'll go back to your bad ways. But that doesn't matter to me any more. As long as you go far away, where I won't hear anything more of you. As long as you do that— Because as far as I'm concerned, you aren't my son any more. I've cursed the blood you got from me. My part of it I've cursed. I said, 'Let the blood I gave him rot in his kidneys.' I said it when I heard you'd taken to the roads, robbing and killing people— Good people. My old friend Tranquilino, for instance. The one who baptized you. The one who gave you your name. Even he had the bad luck to run into you. From that time on I said, 'That one cannot be my son.'

"See if you can't see something now. Or hear something. You'll have to do it from up there because I feel deaf."

"I don't see anything."

"Too bad for you, Ignacio."

"I'm thirsty."

"You'll have to stand it. We must be near now. Because it's now very late at night they must've turned out the lights in the town. But at least you should hear dogs barking. Try to hear."

"Give me some water."

"There's no water here. Just stones. You'll have to stand it. Even if there was water, I wouldn't let you down to drink. There's nobody to help me lift you up again, and I can't do it alone."

"I'm awfully thirsty and sleepy."

"I remember when you were born. You were that way then. You woke up hungry and ate and went back to sleep. Your mother had to give you water, because you'd finished all her milk. You couldn't be filled up. And you were always mad and yelling. I never thought that in time this madness would go to your head. But it did. Your mother, may she rest in peace, wanted you to grow up strong. She

118

thought when you grew up you'd look after her. She only had you. The other child she tried to give birth to killed her. And you would've killed her again, if she'd lived till now."

The man on his back stopped gouging with his knees. His feet began to swing loosely from side to side. And it seemed to the father that Ignacio's head, up there, was shaking as if he were sobbing.

On his hair he felt thick drops fall.

"Are you crying, Ignacio? The memory of your mother makes you cry, doesn't it? But you never did anything for her. You always repaid us badly. Somehow your body got filled with evil instead of affection. And now you see? They've wounded it. What happened to your friends? They were all killed. Only they didn't have anybody. They might well have said, 'We have nobody to be concerned about.' But you, Ignacio?"

At last, the town. He saw roofs shining in the moonlight. He felt his son's weight crushing him as the back of his knees buckled in a final effort. When he reached the first dwelling, he leaned against the wall by the sidewalk. He slipped the body off, dangling, as if it had been wrenched from him.

With difficulty he unpried his son's fingers from around his neck. When he was free, he heard the dogs barking everywhere.

"And you didn't hear them, Ignacio?" he said. "You didn't even help me listen."

Paso del Norte

"I'm going a long way off, Father, that's why I've come to let you know."

"And where are you going, if one may ask?"

"I'm going up North."

"And why up there? Don't you have your business here? Aren't you still in the pig-buying business?"

"I was. But not any more. It doesn't bring in anything. Last week we didn't make enough to eat and the week before we ate pure weeds. We're hungry, Father; you can't even realize that because you have it so good."

"What are you saying?"

"That we're hungry. You don't feel it. You sell your skyrockets and firecrackers and gun powder and you make out all right with that. As long as there are fiestas, your money comes pouring in; but it's not the same for me, Father. Nobody's raising pigs now during this season. And if they do raise them, well they eat them.

Paso del Norte

And if they sell them, they sell them at a steep price. And there's no money to buy them with anyway. The business folded up, Father."

"And what the devil are you going to do up North?"

"Well, make money. You know Carmelo came back rich, even brought back a phonograph, and he charges five centavos to listen to the music. Five centavos for every number, from a Cuban dance to that Anderson woman who sings sad songs—the same for all of them—and he makes good money and they even line up to listen. So you see, you just have to go and come back. That's why I'm going."

"And where are you going to leave your wife and kids?"

"Well, that's why I've come to tell you, so you'll look after them."

"And who do you think I am, your wet nurse? If you go, let God take care of them. I can't raise kids any more; raising you and your sister, may she rest in peace, was more than enough for me. From now on I don't want any troubles. As the saying goes: 'If the bell doesn't ring, it's because there's no clapper'."

"I don't know what to say to you, Father; I don't even recognize you. What have I got out of your raising me? Just pure work. No sooner did you bring me into the world than I had to shift for myself. You didn't even teach me the fireworks trade, so I wouldn't be in competition with you. You put some pants and a shirt on me and put me out on the street to learn to live on my own and you almost threw me out of your house with just the clothes on my back. Now look at the results: we're starving to death. Your daughter-in-law and grandchildren and your son here, as they say, all your descendants, are about to kick the bucket and fall over dead. And what makes me so mad is that it's from hunger. Do you think that's fair and square?"

"And what the devil is it to me? What did you get married for? You left the house and didn't even ask my permission."

"I did that because you never thought Tránsito was a good woman. You ran her down every time I brought her home, and remember, you didn't even look at her the first time she came. 'Look, Papa, this is the girl I'm going to get hitched up with.' You started making up verses saying you knew her intimately, as if she was a woman of the streets. And you said a bunch of things that I didn't even understand. That's why I haven't brought her back. So you shouldn't hold any grudge against me for that. Now I just want you to take care of her for me, because I'm serious about going. There's nothing for me to do here, and not any way to find something to do."

"That's a lot of bunk. You work to eat, and eat to live. Learn from my wisdom. I'm old and I don't complain. When I was young, well, I don't have to tell you; I even had enough to pay for women. Work brings in enough for everything and especially for the body's needs. The trouble is, you're a fool. And don't tell me I taught you that."

"But you brought me into the world. And you should've got me started on the road, and not just turn me out like a horse to pasture."

"You were pretty good-sized when you left home. Or maybe you expect me to support you forever? Only lizards look for the same hole to crawl into till they die. Say that it went well with you and that you knew a woman and had children; some others haven't even had that in their life, but have come and gone like the waters of the rivers, without leaving a trace."

"You didn't even teach me to make up verses, since you knew them. If I'd just had that I might've earned something, amusing people the way you do. And the day I asked you to teach me you said to me, 'Go and sell eggs, that brings in more.' And at first I sold eggs and then chickens and later pigs, and even that didn't go badly, if I may say so. But money runs out; the children come and they drink it down like water and then there's none left for the business and nobody wants to give you credit. I already told you, last week we ate weeds, and this week, well not even that. That's why I'm going. And I'm sad to be going, Father, though you won't believe it, because I love my children, not like you who just raised them and ran them off."

"Learn this, son: in each new nest, one must leave an egg. When the wings of old age begin to brush you, you will learn how to live, you'll find out that your children leave you, that they aren't grateful for anything, that they eat up even your memory."

"That's pure nonsense."

"Maybe so, but it's the truth."

"I haven't forgotten you, as you see."

"You come looking for me when you need me. If everything went all right with you, you'd forget about me. Since your mother died, I've been lonesome; when your sister died, I was more lonesome; when you left I saw that I was left alone forever. Now you come and want to stir up my feelings, but you don't know that it's harder to revive a dead man than give life again. Learn something. Traveling the roads teaches a lot. Scrub yourself with your own scrub brush, that's what you should do."

"Then you won't take care of them for me?"

"Just leave them, nobody dies of hunger."

"Tell me if you'll do this for me; I don't want to go without being sure."

"How many are there?"

"Just three boys and two girls and the daughter-in-law, who is still real young."

"Real screwed out, you mean."

"I was her first. She was a virgin. She's a good woman. Be kind to her, Father."

"And when will you return?"

"Soon, Father. As soon as I get the money together I'll come back. I'll pay you double for what you do for them. Just feed them, that's all I ask you."

From the ranches the people came down to the villages; the people of the villages went to the cities. In the cities the people got lost, vanished among the people. "Do you know where they'll give me work?" "Yes, go to Ciudad Juárez. I'll pass you for two hundred pesos. Look for Mr. So and So and tell him I sent you. But don't tell anybody." "Okay, mister, tomorrow I'll bring the money."

"Listen, they say that at Nonoalco they need people for unloading the trains."

"And they pay?"

"Of course, two pesos for twenty-five pounds."

"Are you serious? Yesterday I unloaded about a ton of bananas behind the Merced market and they gave me what I ate. It turned out that I had robbed them and they didn't pay me a thing and they even reported me to the police."

"The railroads are serious. They're not the same thing. Let's see if you're brave enough."

"Why not!"

"Tomorrow I'll wait for you."

And yes, we unloaded merchandise from the trains from morning till night and there was still work left for another day. They

paid us. I counted the money: seventy-four pesos. If only every day were like this.

"Mister, here are your two hundred pesos."

"Fine. I'm going to give you a slip of paper for our friend in Ciudad Juárez. Don't lose it. He'll pass you across the border and besides you'll have your contract. Here's his address and telephone number so you can locate him quicker. No, you're not going to Texas. Have you ever heard of Oregon? Well, tell him you want to go to Oregon. To harvest apples, that's it, no cotton fields. I can see you're a smart man. There you go see Fernández. Don't you know him? Well, ask for him. And if you don't want to harvest apples, you can lay railroad ties. That pays more and lasts longer. You'll come back with lots of dollars. Don't lose the card."

"Father, they killed us."

"Who?"

"Us. When we crossed the river. They peppered us with bullets until they killed all of us."

"Where?"

"There, in El Paso del Norte, while they flashed the lights on us when we were crossing the river."

"Why?"

"Well, I didn't know, Father. You remember Estanislado? He's the one who got me to go up there. He told me how we could manage things and first we went to Mexico City and then from there to El Paso. And we were crossing the river when they shot at us with their rifles. I turned back because he said to me, 'Get me out of here, pal, don't leave me.' And then he was already on his back, his body all full of holes, and gone slack. I dragged him the best

I could, tugging him, trying to keep to one side of the lights they were flashing, looking for us. I said, 'Are you alive?' and he answered, 'Get me out of here, pal.' And then he said to me, 'They got me.' One of my arms was smashed by a bullet and the bone stuck out at my elbow. That's why I grabbed him with my good hand and said to him, 'Hold on tight here.' But he died on me by the shore, near the lights of a place they call Ojinaga, on this side, among the river reeds that continued combing the river as if nothing had happened.

"I pulled him up on the bank and said to him, "Are you still alive?' And he didn't answer me. I fought to revive Estanislado until dawn; I rubbed him and massaged his lungs to get him to breathe, but not a peep came from him.

"The immigration officer came up to me in the afternoon.

" 'Hey, you, what you doing here?'

" 'Why, I'm looking after this dead fellow.'

" 'Did you kill him?'

" 'No, sergeant,' I said.

" 'I'm no sergeant. Then who did?'

"As he had on a uniform with those little eagles I figured he was in the army, and he was carrying such a big pistol I had no doubts about it.

"Then he asked me again, 'Well who then?' He kept at me until he grabbed me by the hair and I didn't put up any fight, because I couldn't defend myself with my bum elbow.

"I said to him, 'Don't hit me; I've only got one good arm.'

"That made him stop.

" 'What happened? Tell me,' he said.

" 'Well, they shot us last night. We were going along real happy like, whistling away we were so pleased to be going to the other side when smack in the middle of the river the firing broke loose. And nobody could stop it. This fellow and me were the only ones who managed to get away, and only partly, because look, he's kicked the bucket too.'

" 'And who were the ones who did the shooting?'

" 'Well, we didn't even see them. They just turned their lights on us, and bang, bang, we heard the rifle shots until I felt a wrench in my elbow and heard this guy say, "Get me out of the water, pal." But it wouldn't have done us any good to have seen them.'

" 'Then they must have been the Apaches.'

" 'What Apaches?'

" 'Oh, some people called that who live on the other side.'

" 'But aren't they Texans on the other side?'

" 'Yes, but you have no idea how full of Apaches it is. I'm going to talk to Ojinaga to get them to pick up your friend and you get ready to go back to your home. Where you from? You shouldn't have left there. Have you got any money?'

" 'I took this little bit from the dead man. Let's see if it'll get me through.'

" 'I have some funds for those repatriated. I'll give you your fare; but if I see you here again, I'll just let you look out for yourself. I don't like to see the same face twice. Go on now, on your way!'

"And I came and here I am, Father, to tell you about it."

"That's what you get for being a sucker and a fool. And you'll see when you go to your house, you'll see what you gained by going."

"Did something bad happen? Did one of my kids die?"

"Tránsito ran off with a mule driver. You said she was real good, didn't you? Your kids are here in the back asleep. And you can go look for some place to spend the night, because I sold your house to pay for the expenses. And you still owe me thirty pesos, which the title cost."

"Okay, Father, I'm not going to refuse to pay you. Maybe tomorrow I'll find some work around here so I can pay you all I owe you. In what direction did you say the mule driver went with Tránsito?"

"Over there. I didn't pay any attention."

"Then I'll be back soon; I'm going after her."

"And which way are you going?"

"Well, that way, Father, there where you say she went."

Anacleto Morones

Old women, daughters of the devil! I saw them coming all together in a procession. Dressed in black, sweating like mules under the hot sun. I saw them from a long way off as if they were a string of mules raising the dust. Their faces now ashen with dust. All of them black. They came along the Amula road, singing while they prayed in the heat, with their large black scapularies on which the sweat from their faces fell in big drops.

I saw them arrive and I hid myself. I knew what they were up to and who they were looking for. That's why I hurried to hide out in the back of the yard, running with my pants already in my hands.

But they came in and found me. They said, "Holy Mother of God!"

I was squatting down on a stone without doing anything, just sitting there with my pants down, so they would see me and not come close. But all they said was "Holy Mother of God," and kept right on coming.

Nasty old women! They ought to be ashamed of themselves! They crossed themselves and came right up to me, all pressed together, in a bunch, streaming sweat and with their hair plastered to their faces as if it had been raining.

"We came to see you, Lucas Lucatero. From Amula we came, just to see you. Nearby they told us you were at home; but we didn't figure you would be way back here doing this. We thought you'd come out here to feed the chickens; that's why we came in. We came to see you."

Those old hags! Old and ugly as burro saddle sores!

"Tell me what you want!" I said to them, while I buttoned up my pants and they covered their eyes so as not to see.

"We have come on a mission. We've looked for you in Santo Santiago and in Santa Inés, but they informed us you didn't live there any more, that you'd moved to this ranch. And so we came here. We're from Amula."

I already knew where they were from and who they were; I could have even recited their names, but I let on that I didn't know.

"Well now, Lucas Lucatero, finally we've found you, thank God."

I invited them onto the porch and brought out some chairs for them to sit on. I asked them if they were hungry or if they would like something to wet their tongues, even if it was just a jug of water.

They sat down, wiping off the sweat with their scapularies.

"No thank you," they said. "We didn't come to bother you. We came on a mission. You know me, don't you, Lucas Lucatero?" one of them asked me.

"Maybe," I said to her. "I think I've seen you somewhere. You couldn't be Pancha Fregoso, who let herself be carried off by Homobono Ramos?"

"Yes, I am, but nobody carried me off. That was just pure evil talk. The two of us got lost looking for berries. I'm a church member and I would never have let him—"

"What, Pancha?"

"Ah, what an evil mind you have, Lucas. You still have the habit of going around accusing people of crimes. But, now that you know me, I want to speak up to tell you why we've come."

"Wouldn't you even like a glass of water?" I asked them again.

"Don't bother. But since you beg us so much we won't turn you down."

I brought them a jug of water flavored with myrtle and they drank it down. Then I brought them another and they drank that one too. Then I put a jug of water from the river down near them. They left it there to drink after a while, because, according to them, they would get very thirsty when their digestion started working.

Ten women, seated in a row, with their black dresses filthy with dirt. The daughters of Ponciano, Emiliano, Crescenciano, Toribio the tavernkeeper, and Anastasio the barber.

Old bitches! Not one of them fit for anything. All of them past fifty. Dried up like withered, faded floripondios. No choice among them.

"And what are you looking for?"

"We came to see you."

"You've seen me now. I'm fine. You don't need to worry about me."

"You've come a long way. To this hidden place. Without an address or anyone knowing where you were. We've had quite a time finding you after a lot of asking around."

"I'm not hiding. I'm contented living here, without people to bother me. And what mission brings you here, if one may ask?" I said to them.

"Well, it's about— But don't go to the trouble of fixing us something to eat. We already ate at La Torcacita's house. They fed all of us there. So listen to us now. Sit here facing us so we can all see you and you can hear us."

I was uneasy. I wanted to go out again to the yard. I heard the cackling of the hens and I felt like going out to gather the eggs before the rabbits ate them up.

"I'm going out to gather the eggs," I told them.

"But really, we have already eaten. Don't bother about us."

"I have two rabbits loose out there that eat the eggs. I'll be right back."

And I went out to the yard.

I didn't plan to return. Just go out by the door facing the mountains and leave that bunch of old fools in the lurch.

I glanced at the pile of stones that I had heaped up in a corner and I saw the form of a grave. Then I began to scatter them, throwing them in every direction, making a row here and another there. They were river stones, ball-shaped, and I could throw them a long way. God-damned old women! They had put me to work. I don't know why they got it into their heads to come here.

I quit doing that and went back in.

I gave them the eggs.

"Did you kill the rabbits? We saw you throwing rocks at them. We'll keep the eggs for a little later on. You shouldn't have gone to the trouble."

"They may hatch on your breasts, so you better leave them outside."

"Oh, you Lucas Lucatero you! You're still full of the same old nonsense. As if we were all that hot."

"I don't know anything about that. But outside here it's plenty hot."

What I wanted to do was to keep them indefinitely from bringing up a certain matter. To get them off on another track, while I looked for the way to get rid of them so they wouldn't want to come back. But nothing occurred to me.

I knew they had been looking for me since January, a little after Anacleto Morones disappeared. Of course I had been told that the old women of the Congregation of Amula were on my trail. They were the only ones who could have any interest in Anacleto Morones. And now here they were.

I could keep on conversing with them or winning their favor in some way until night came and they'd have to leave. They wouldn't dare spend the night in my house.

For a moment that subject came up, when Ponciano's daughter said that they wanted to wind up their business soon so they could return early to Amula. Then I made them see they needn't worry about returning, that even if some of them had to sleep on the floor there was more than enough room and pallets there for them. They all said they wouldn't think of it, because what would people say when they found out that they had passed the night all alone with me there. Certainly not.

So the thing to do was to keep on talking with them until night came, getting them to think of something else besides the idea that was buzzing in their heads. I asked one of them, "And what does your husband say?"

"I don't have a husband, Lucas. Don't you remember that I was your sweetheart? I waited and waited for you and all I did was wait. Then I found out you had got married. By that time nobody wanted me."

"And me? What happened was I got mixed up in other affairs that kept me very busy; but there's still time."

"But you're married, Lucas, and no less than with the Holy Child's daughter. Why do you get me all stirred up again? I had even forgotten you."

"But I hadn't. What did you say your name was?"

"Nieves— My name is still Nieves. Nieves García. Don't make me cry, Lucas Lucatero. Just remembering your sweet promises makes me angry."

"Nieves—Nieves. How can I forget you? Why you're something one doesn't forget— You're smooth. I remember. I still feel you here in my arms. Smooth. Soft. The smell of the dress you wore when you came out to see me smelled of camphor. And you snuggled right up to me. You hugged me so tight I almost felt you in my bones. I remember."

"Don't go on saying such things, Lucas. Yesterday I went to confession and you are awakening bad thoughts in me and making me feel like sinning."

"I remember I used to kiss you on the back of your knees. And you said not there, because it tickled. Do you still have dimples on the back of your knees?"

"Better be still, Lucas Lucatero. God will not pardon what you did to me. You will pay dearly for it."

"Did I do anything bad to you? Was I mean to you?"

"I had to throw it away. And don't make me tell about it here in front of people. But so you'll know—I had to throw it away. It was something like a piece of jerky. And why should I love it, if its father was just a shameless good-for-nothing?"

"So that happened? I didn't know. Wouldn't you like to have a little more myrtle water? It won't take me any time to make it. Just wait a moment."

I went out again to the yard to cut myrtle. And there I delayed as long as I could until that woman would get over her bad humor.

When I returned she had left.

"Did she leave?"

"Yes, she left. You made her cry."

"I just wanted to talk with her, just to pass the time. Have you noticed how slow it is in raining here? In Amula it must have already rained, hasn't it?"

"Yes, day before yesterday there was a downpour."

"There is no doubt that Amula is a good place. It rains well and one lived well there. I swear that here the clouds don't even appear. Is Rogaciano still the mayor?"

"Yes, he still is."

"Rogaciano is a good man."

"No, he's evil."

"Maybe you're right. And what news of Edelmiro? Is his drugstore still closed?"

"Edelmiro died. It was a good thing he died, though I shouldn't say it, but he was another evil man. He was among those who said terrible things about Anacleto, the Holy Child. He accused him of being a fortuneteller and a quack and a swindler. He went around saying these things everywhere. But people didn't pay any attention to him and God punished him. He died of rabies."

"Let us hope to God that he is in hell."

"And that the devils don't get tired of heaping firewood on him."

"The same thing happened to Lirio López, the judge, who sided with him and sent the Holy Child to jail."

Now they were the ones doing the talking. I let them talk all they wanted. As long as they let me alone everything would be all right. But suddenly they took a notion to ask me: "Will you come with us?"

"Where?"

"To Amula. That's why we came. To take you with us."

For a moment I felt like going back out to the yard. Slipping out the door that faces the mountain and disappearing. Old hags!

"And what the devil will I do in Amula?"

"We want you to accompany us in our prayers. All us women who were followers of the Holy Child Anacleto have started a novena to ask that he be made a saint. You are his son-in-law and we need you to serve as a witness. The priest recommended that we bring someone who had known him well and for some time back, before he became famous for his miracles. And who better than you, who lived by his side and can point out better than anyone else his works of mercy. That's why we need you, so you'll help us out in this campaign."

Old hags! They should have said so earlier.

"I can't go," I told them. "I have nobody to take care of my house."

"Two girls will stay here to tend to it; we've thought of that. Besides, there's your wife."

"I haven't got a wife any more."

"What about your wife, the daughter of the Holy Child Anacleto?"

"She left. I ran her off."

"But that can't be, Lucas Lucatero. The poor thing must be suffering. She was so good. And so young and pretty. Where did you send her, Lucas? We'll be satisfied if at least you have put her in the convent of the Repentant Women."

"I didn't put her anywhere. I ran her off. And I'm sure she's not with the Repentant Women; she was too fond of being loose and bawdy. She must have taken that road, unbuttoning pants."

"We don't believe you, Lucas, not for a minute do we believe you. She's probably right here, shut up in some room of this house, saying her prayers. You were always quite a liar and even a false witness. Remember, Lucas, Hermelindo's poor daughters, who even had to go to El Grullo because people whistled at them the song of 'The Pigeons' every time they showed their faces on the street, and only because you invented gossip. One can't believe anything you say, Lucas Lucatero."

"Well then, there's no reason for me to go to Amula."

"You'll confess first and then everything will be all right. When was the last time you confessed?"

"Uh! About fifteen years ago. Since the time when the Cristeros were going to shoot me. They shoved a gun in my back and made me kneel in front of the priest, and I confessed to things there that I hadn't even done yet."

"If it weren't for the fact that you're the Holy Child's son-in-law we wouldn't come looking for you, and, besides, we wouldn't ask anything of you. You've always been a real devil, Lucas Lucatero."

"For some reason I was Anacleto Morones' helper. He was the living devil himself."

"Don't blaspheme."

"You didn't know him."

"We knew him as a saint."

"But not as a seller of saints."

"What are you saying, Lucas?"

"You didn't know that, but he used to sell saints. In the fairs. At church doorways. I carried the big bundle for him. And there we went the two of us, one behind the other, from village to village. He in front of me carrying the bundle with the novenas of San Pantaleón, San Ambrosio and San Pascual, which weighed at least seventy-five pounds.

"One day we met some pilgrims. Anacleto was kneeling on top of an ant hill, showing me how by biting your tongue the ants don't sting you. Then the pilgrims passed. They saw him. They stopped to look at that strange sight. They asked, 'How can you be on top of the ant hill without the ants stinging you?'

"Then he crossed his arms and began to tell them how he'd just come from Rome, from where he brought a message and was the bearer of a splinter of wood from the Holy Cross on which Christ was crucified.

"They lifted him up then and there in their arms. They carried him on a litter to Amula. And there it was the limit; the people prostrated themselves before him and asked him for miracles. This was the beginning. And I was open-mouthed watching him fool that mass of pilgrims who came to see him."

"You're just full of talk, and worse than that, you're blasphemous. Who were you before you knew him? A swineherd. And he made you rich. He gave you what you have. And even for that you can't manage to speak well of him. Ingrate."

"Well, I'm grateful to him for stopping my hunger, but that doesn't take away the fact that he was the living devil. He still is, wherever he may be."

"He's in heaven. Among the angels. That's where he is, whether you like it or not."

"I heard he was in jail."

"That's a long time ago. He escaped from there. He disappeared without leaving a trace. Now he's in heaven in body and soul. And from up there he's blessing us. Girls! Kneel down! Let us pray the 'We are penitent, Lord,' so the Holy Child will intervene for us."

And those old women knelt down, at each paternoster kissing the scapular where the portrait of Anacleto Morones was embroidered.

It was three o'clock in the afternoon.

I took advantage of that time to go to the kitchen and eat some bean tacos. When I came out only five women were left.

"What happened to the others?" I asked them.

Pancha, the four hairs of her mustache bristling, said to me, "They left. They don't want to have to deal with you."

"All the better. The fewer the burros the more feed there is. Do you want some more myrtle water?"

One of them, Filomena, who had been quiet the whole time and who was called the Dead One, rushed over to one of my flowerpots and, putting her finger down her throat, brought up all the myrtle water she had swallowed, mixed in with pieces of sausage and fruit seeds: "I don't even want your myrtle water, you're so blasphemous. I don't want a thing from you."

And she placed the egg I had given her on her chair.

"I don't even want your eggs! It's best I leave."

Now only four were left.

"I feel like vomiting too," said Pancha. "But I won't. We must take you to Amula someway or other. You are the only one who can testify to the saintliness of the Holy Child. He will soften your soul. We have already placed his image in the church and it would not be right to throw it out into the street through your fault."

"Look for somebody else. I don't want any part of this business."

"You were almost his son. You inherited the fruit of his saintliness. He put his eyes on you to perpetuate him. He gave you his daughter."

"Yes, but he gave her to me already perpetuated."

"Good heavens, what things you say, Lucas Lucatero."

"But it's true, he gave her to me when she was at least four months along."

"But she smelled saintly."

"She stank. She liked to show her belly to everybody who came by, so they'd see it was flesh. She showed them her bulging stomach, purplish with the swelling of the child she carried inside. And they laughed. They thought it was funny. She was a shameless hussy, that's what Anacleto Morones' daughter was—"

"Blasphemous one. You have no right to say such things. We are going to give you a scapulary to chase away the devil."

"—She went off with one of those fellows. They say he loved her. He just told her, 'I'll dare to be the father of your child!' And she went with him."

"She was the fruit of the Holy Child. A girl child. And you received her as a gift. You were the master of that richness born in sanctity."

"Nonsense!"

"What's that?"

"Inside Anacleto Morones' daughter was Anacleto Morones' grandchild."

"You invented that to accuse him of evil things. You've always been one for making up tales."

"Is that so? And what about all the other girls? He left this part of the country without virgins, always seeing to it that a maiden watched over his sleep."

"He did that out of purity. So he wouldn't dirty himself with sin. He wanted to surround himself with innocence so he wouldn't stain his soul."

"That's what you think because he didn't call on you."

"He called on me," said the one whose name was Melquiades. "I watched over his sleep."

"And what happened?"

"Nothing. Except that his miraculous hands wrapped themselves around me in that hour when you begin to feel the cold. And I thanked him for the warmth of his body, but nothing else."

"That's because you were old. He liked them young and tender, liked to hear their bones breaking, to hear them snap as if they were peanut shells."

"You're a cursed atheist, Lucas Lucatero. One of the worst."

Now The Orphan was talking, the one who was forever blubbering. The oldest of the lot. Her eyes were filled with tears and her hands trembled: "I'm an orphan and he consoled me; I found my father and mother again in him. He spent the whole night caressing me so I wouldn't feel so bad."

She shed tears.

"You don't have any reason for crying then," I said to her.

"But my parents died and left me alone. An orphan at that age when it's so difficult to find help. The only happy night I spent was with the Holy Child Anacleto in his consoling arms. And now you say bad things about him."

"He was a saint."

"A good, kind man."

"We hoped you would continue his work. You inherited it all."

"He left me a sack of vices of all the devils put together. A wild woman. Not as old as you, but pretty wild. It's a good thing she left. I myself held the door open for her."

"Heretic! You make up pure heresies."

Now only two old women were left. The others had been leaving, one after another, making the sign of the cross over me and withdrawing, promising to return with the exorcisms.

"You aren't going to deny that the Holy Child Anacleto brought about miracles," said Anastasio's daughter. "You surely aren't going to deny that."

"To beget children is no miracle. That was his strong point."

"He cured my husband of syphilis."

"I didn't know you had a husband. Aren't you the daughter of the barber Anastasio? Tacho's daughter is single, as far as I know."

"I am single, but I have a husband. It's one thing to be a señorita and another to be single. You know that. And I'm not a señorita, but I am single."

"Doing that at your age, Micaela."

"I had to. What good did I get out of living as a señorita? I'm a woman. And a woman is born to give what is given her."

"You use the very words of Anacleto Morones."

"Yes, he advised me to do it to get rid of my liver trouble. So I did. Being fifty years old and a virgin is a sin."

"Anacleto Morones told you that."

"Yes, he did. But we've come for another reason, for you to go with us and certify that he was a saint."

"And why not me?"

"You've never brought about a miracle. He cured my husband. It's clear to me. Have you ever cured anybody of syphilis?"

"No, and I don't know what it's like."

"It's something like gangrene. He got purple and his body full of chilblains. He couldn't sleep any more. He said that he saw everything colored red as if he were at the gates of hell. And then he felt stabs of pain that made him flinch. Then we went to see the Holy Child Anacleto and he cured him. He burned him with a flaming reed and he rubbed his own saliva on his wounds, and, there you are, his sickness went away. Now tell me if that wasn't a miracle."

"He must have had measles. They cured me too with saliva when I was a little kid."

"Like I said before. You're a hopeless atheist."

"I have the consolation that Anacleto Morones was worse than me."

"He treated you like his son. And you still dare— I'd best not keep on listening to you. I'm leaving. Are you staying, Pancha?"

"I'll stay a little longer. I'll fight the last battle alone."

"Listen, Francisca, now they've all gone you'll stay and sleep with me, won't you?"

"God forbid. What would people think? What I want to do is to convince you."

"Well, let's convince each other. After all, what have you got to lose? You're too old for anybody to pay any attention to you or do you that favor."

"But people talk so, and they'll think bad things."

"Let them think what they want. What difference does it make? Your name is Pancha anyway."

"All right, I'll stay with you, but only until dawn. And only if you promise to go with me to Amula, so I can tell them I passed the night begging and pleading with you. If not, how will I manage it?"

"Okay. But first cut off those hairs over your lips. I'll bring you the scissors."

"How you make fun of me, Lucas Lucatero! You spend your life looking at my defects. Leave my mustache in peace. That way they won't suspect anything."

"All right, if that's what you want."

When it got dark she helped me put up the chicken roost and gather together the rocks I had scattered all over the yard, piling them up in the corner where they were before.

She had no idea that Anacleto Morones was buried there. Or that he died the same day he escaped from jail and came here demanding I return his property to him.

He arrived saying: "Sell everything and give me the money, because I need to take a trip up North. I'll write you from there and we'll go into business together again."

"Why don't you take your daughter along?" I said to him. "That's all I have left of what you say is yours. You even tricked me with your double dealing."

"You two will follow me later, when I let you know my whereabouts. There we'll settle accounts."

"It would be much better to settle them here and now. So that we're squared up."

"I'm not in the mood for playing now," he said to me. "Give me what is mine. How much money have you got salted away?"

"I have some, but I'm not going to give it to you. I've gone through hell with your shameless daughter. Consider yourself well paid by my keeping her."

He got angry. He stamped his feet on the ground and insisted he had to leave.

"May you rest in peace, Anacleto Morones!" I said when I buried him, and at each trip back from the river loaded with stones to throw on top of him, "You won't get out of here even though you use all your tricks."

And now Pancha was helping me put the stones over him again without suspecting that underneath lay Anacleto and that I was doing that for fear he would come out of his grave to give me a bad time again. He was so full of tricks, I had no doubt he would find some way to come to life and get out of there.

"Pile on more rocks, Pancha, here in this corner; I don't like to see my yard all rocky."

Afterwards she said to me, when it was already dawn, "You're a flop, Lucas Lucatero. You aren't the least bit affectionate. Do you know who was really loving?"

"Who?"

"The Holy Child Anacleto. He knew how to make love."